Animal Ark

Special two-in-one edition

Cub in the Cupboard
Owl in the Office

Animal Ark series

LUCY DANIELS
Cub
—*in the*—
Cupboard

Illustrations by Shelagh McNicholas

**Hodder
Children's
Books**

a division of Hodder Headline

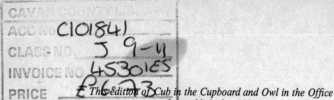
This edition of *Cub in the Cupboard and Owl in the Office*
first published in 1995
ISBN 0 340 65353 1

*Special thanks to C. J. Hall, B.Vet.Med., M.R.C.V.S. for reviewing
the veterinary information contained in this book*

Cub in the Cupboard
Special thanks to Helen Magee

Animal Ark is a trademark of Working Partners Ltd
Text Copyright © Working Partners Ltd 1994
Illustrations copyright © Shelagh McNicholas 1994
Created by Working Partners Ltd, London W6 0QT
Original series created by Ben M. Baglio

First published as a single volume in Great Britain in 1994
by Hodder Children's Books

The right of Lucy Daniels to be identified as the Author of the Work
has been asserted by her in accordance with the Copyright, Designs
and Patents Act 1988.

20 19 18 17

A catalogue record for this book is available from the British Library

Typeset by Avon Dataset Ltd, Bidford-on-Avon, B50 4JH

Printed and bound in Great Britain by
Clays Ltd, St Ives plc

Hodder Children's Books
a division of Hodder Headline
338 Euston Road
London NW1 3BH

One

The sound of bells floated on the air as Mandy Hope and her friend, James Hunter, crested the hill above Welford. They halted their bikes and looked down on the scene below. Welford lay spread out before them like a toy village.

'Look, there's Mr Hardy coming out of the Fox and Goose,' said Mandy pointing to the pub where the village's two streets crossed.

'And there's Animal Ark,' said James.

Animal Ark was Mandy's home. It was also her mum and dad's veterinary practice. 'Look, Simon is just arriving,' James went on.

Mandy looked down on the old, stone cottage

with the modern extension at the back. A fair-haired, young man was just turning the corner of the house. Simon was the practice nurse at Animal Ark.

The bells rang out even louder and she switched her attention to the church. 'Gran and Grandad should be back soon,' she said to James. Mandy's grandparents were on a tour of the Border country of the north of England.

'Back from the wilds of Northumberland,' James said, smiling. 'They're real travellers, your gran and grandad, ever since they got that camper van.'

Mandy laughed. 'Gran certainly is,' she said. 'We got a postcard from her. They've been doing a lot of hill walking. But sometimes I think Grandad would be happier staying in Welford with his vegetables and his bell-ringing.'

Another peal from the church tower startled the rooks nesting in the trees around the church. They rose into the air in a great cloud of black, beating wings.

'Walter Pickard seems to be doing all right with those bells without any help,' said James.

Mandy laughed again. 'Grandad says he gets carried away sometimes.' She lifted her head and let the fresh spring breeze cool her cheeks. They were hot from the effort of cycling to the top of the hill.

'Race you to the bottom of the hill,' James said.

Mandy swung her head round, short, fair hair blowing across her eyes. She shook it back and grinned at James. He shoved his glasses more securely up on to his nose and grinned back at her.

'Where's the finishing line?' she said.

James looked thoughtful. 'The bridge over the stream at the bottom of the hill,' he said. 'By Monkton Spinney.'

'OK,' said Mandy. 'You're on!' And she set off, flying down the hill, free-wheeling as the steepness of the slope increased.

'Wait for me!' James shouted, but she hardly heard him.

The wind flattened Mandy's jumper against her chest and her hair fluttered free of her face. Above her the sky was blue, around her the countryside was fresh and green. It was one of those magical spring days when all was right with the world.

They were neck and neck as they approached the bridge where the road narrowed. Mandy put on an extra spurt and drew just ahead of James as they reached the bridge.

'I won, I won!' she cried as she slowed her bike to a halt at the other end of the bridge.

James swerved and came to a sliding halt beside her. 'Only just,' he said.

They stood there for a moment astride their bikes, catching their breath. The air was still and warm down in the shelter of the valley. They could hear small sounds. The call of a bird in the wood, the rustle of some small creature in the undergrowth and a fish splashing as it surfaced right below the bridge.

Here, the water was smooth and free running but further along, as it flowed through the wood, it became rougher. Mandy gazed at the water. Then she started.

'What was that?' she said.

James turned to her as she swung her bike round. 'What?' he said slewing his own bike round and stopping just in front of her.

Mandy frowned. 'I heard something,' she said. 'Down there.' She pointed down towards the little wood on their right.

James looked where she was pointing. 'In Monkton Spinney?' he said. Then he looked at her face. 'What kind of noise?'

Mandy shook her head and pushed the hair out

of her eyes. 'I don't know,' she said. 'It sounded like a cry.'

'Like a baby?' said James. He was clearly puzzled.

Mandy looked down towards the spinney. Through the trees, she could see the rush of water as the stream tumbled through the rocks which edged the steep banks. The water gleamed silver in the sunlight. Then the sound came again; a thin cry swept away on the breeze.

'There,' said Mandy. 'There it is again.'

James bit his lip. 'It doesn't sound like a baby to me,' he said. 'More like an animal.'

'Yes,' said Mandy. 'It *is* an animal. It's an animal in trouble.' She swung one long leg over her bike and stood beside it, her face intent. 'We've got to find it, James. We've got to help it.'

James looked at her. There was no arguing with Mandy when she thought there was an animal in trouble. Not that James wanted to argue. He loved animals nearly as much as Mandy did. 'What about your mum?' he said. 'We promised her we'd meet her at The Riddings at two. It's nearly that now.'

Mandy bit her lip. She and James had been on their way to see Patch, a kitten the Spry sisters had adopted from them a while ago. Mrs Hope had said she would meet them there. The Sprys were elderly ladies and they didn't like coming into Animal Ark with Patch. But Mrs Hope didn't mind making calls. Patch meant so much to the sisters. Having him had really changed their lives. Before they adopted the kitten they had been real hermits. Now they were beginning to come out of their shells.

'We might miss her,' said James. 'And then you wouldn't get to see Patch. The Sprys let hardly anybody into that big house of theirs.'

Mandy frowned. It was true. And she hadn't seen Patch since the sisters took him in. But that cry had sounded serious. She made up her mind.

'It can't be helped,' she said. 'Mum will understand. After all she's a vet. She'd do the same if she thought she could help an animal in trouble.'

Just then another cry floated up from the wood – more piercing this time, a cry of real pain. Mandy strained her eyes to see into the wood but the shadows were dark beneath the trees. It was hard to see. She turned back to James but he was already off his bike and wheeling it to the side of the road.

'That sounded bad,' he said. 'What do you think it is?'

Mandy shook her head as she wheeled her bike off the bridge and leaned it against the low dry-stone wall that bordered the road. 'I don't know,' she said. 'It sounds a bit like a dog in pain.'

James frowned. 'Well, if anything happened to Blackie I'd want somebody to investigate it,' he said. Blackie was James's Labrador.

Mandy nodded. 'Then let's go!' she said.

She was off, long legs leaping the wall, feet flying as she sped through the bracken towards the little wood.

'Hey, wait for me!' said James but Mandy didn't hear. Hair flying, feet leaping the tussocks of grass, she covered the distance between the road and the wood in long, easy strides. When it came to an animal in trouble there was only one thing on Mandy's mind – helping.

She reached the wood out of breath with James crashing behind her. 'Shh,' she said. 'We don't want to frighten it. Where do you think it is?'

James looked round. The little wood was quiet except for the sound of their breathing and the splash of water on rocks. A blackbird trilled but there was no other sound – no sound to guide them to where an animal was in pain. Then, sharp and clear it came again – a long drawn out cry echoing into the stillness of the wood. It died away as if whatever made it was growing weaker.

Mandy turned swiftly to her right. 'Over there,' she said, pointing down towards a deep depression in the ground where the wood sloped away towards the rocks. James made to run but Mandy stopped him. 'We'll have to be very quiet,' she said. 'A hurt animal can do itself even more harm if it's frightened.'

Slowly, carefully, they crept down through the wood towards the hollow. There were ferns growing all down the sides of the slope, covering anything that might be down there. The cry came once more and Mandy parted a clump of ferns and looked into the hollow. At first she couldn't see anything. Then she saw a movement, a reddish-brown something stirring the ferns at the bottom of the hollow.

'Down there,' she said.

As quietly as they could, they made their way down the slope until they came to the place where the sound had come from. Gently, Mandy parted the ferns. For a moment she stood, unable to move.

'What is it?' said James from behind.

Mandy turned a white face to him and just shook her head. She didn't seem able to speak.

James came to stand beside her. At their feet, not a metre away, lay a fox, its eyes glazed with pain and fear. Its leg was caught in a steel trap, the blood dried and matted now.

As they stood there the fox lifted its head slightly and looked at them. Its eyes flickered in terror and again it gave the cry they had heard, but weaker now. It tried to squirm free of the trap to get away from them and there was another fresh spurt of blood from its wound.

Mandy could feel its terror. She reached out a hand and laid it on the fox's side. Its fur was the colour of autumn leaves. 'Don't,' she said. 'Don't struggle. You'll only make it worse.'

The sound of her voice, gentle and soothing, seemed to calm the terrified animal. 'We'll get you out,' Mandy was saying when James took her elbow.

'Look, Mandy,' he said. 'Look!' His voice sounded funny.

Mandy looked where he was pointing. Huddled beneath the fox where the ferns hid them from sight were four newborn cubs, their fur glistening, their eyes tightly closed. Their fur was dark and woolly, and they looked more like Alsatian puppies than foxes.

Mandy gasped. 'They can't be more than an hour old,' she said.

James nodded and gulped as Mandy bent to the

cubs. When she didn't say anything more he said, 'What's the matter?'

Mandy lifted her face to his. Tears were streaming down it. 'They're dead, James,' she said. 'The cubs are dead. The vixen must have given birth early and now her cubs are dead.'

James swallowed hard. 'At least we can try to save her,' he said. 'Come on, Mandy.'

He was down on his knees beside the trap, trying to force the cruel steel jaws apart. In a second Mandy was beside him, her face still stained with tears but hope in her voice. 'The trap hasn't closed completely. Look, there's a stone wedged in it – here between

the teeth.' James looked. The trap had sprung nearly together but a stone had been caught in it, wedging it slightly open.

'If we can just move the vixen's leg a couple of centimetres we can get it through the gap,' Mandy said.

'Be careful,' said James. 'If you dislodge that stone the trap will spring tighter.'

Mandy looked at the steel jaws of the trap with their sharp, jagged edges. She shivered. One wrong move and the thing would spring really tightly shut and the vixen's leg would be shattered.

They worked very gently, easing the vixen's leg millimetre by millimetre until they got it in position.

'Now!' said Mandy and together they lifted the leg clear of the teeth of the trap. The vixen yelped and tried to snarl at them but she was too weak to do anything. Her deep brown eyes were full of pain. The leg came free and Mandy heaved a sigh of relief.

Feeling her freedom, the vixen tried to stand and, as she did so, she nudged the trap. The stone fell and the trap's jaws sprang together like a vice. The sound made Mandy jump with fright. She stared at the trap in horror. Mandy had always hated such things, but it wasn't until that moment that she fully realised just how cruel they were.

'What have you done to your hand?' James said.

Mandy looked down. There was blood on her hand.

'Oh,' she said. 'That must have happened when the trap sprang closed.'

James looked worried. 'You'd better put something round it to stop the blood,' he said.

Mandy pulled out a handkerchief and wiped her hand with it. 'It's nothing,' she said. 'It's just a graze.'

'Does it hurt?' said James.

Mandy turned to him. 'As if that matters. We did it, James. We got the vixen out of the trap!'

James looked down. 'She looks pretty weak,' he said. 'What are we going to do?'

There was no answer.

'Mandy?' he said.

But Mandy was staring at the vixen as she edged nearer to her poor dead cubs, dragging her wounded leg behind her. They watched as she nuzzled and nudged at the cubs, licking one and then another. Then she seemed to concentrate on one cub, nudging, licking, nuzzling. Mandy felt the prick of tears. 'Poor thing,' she said. 'Doesn't she know they're dead?'

Then incredibly, as they watched, there was a movement. The cub the vixen was concentrating on stirred and moved and tried to nuzzle blindly towards its mother. The vixen nudged it into position and it began to feed.

Mandy looked at the vixen. She was weak with loss of blood and the effort of dragging herself to her little cub. But instinct had triumphed over hurt and pain. She had thought of her cubs first. Her eyes were closed now but the cub was feeding, its black furry sides heaving.

Mandy turned a shining face on James. 'One of the cubs is alive,' she said. 'Alive, James!'

James pursed his lips. 'What about the vixen though?' he said. 'She looks pretty weak.'

Mandy bit her lip. 'We can't just leave them here,' she said. 'They would never survive. James, you've got to go to the Sprys and get Mum. Tell her to come as quickly as she can. I'll stay here and keep watch in case . . .'

'In case what?' said James.

Mandy's face set. 'Nothing,' she said. 'Just go, James – and hurry.'

She watched him go, her mouth still set in a grim line. She wasn't going to leave mother and child – not when they still had a chance to survive. And she had to stay – in case whoever had set the trap came back and finished off their dirty work. Mandy sat there, stroking the vixen's deep red coat. She watched the cub struggling for life and wondered who could have been so cruel.

Two

It was the longest half-hour of Mandy's life. She sat watching over the vixen and her cub until the little animal finished feeding and crept even closer to his mother's side.

Mandy looked at the vixen. Her eyes were still closed. Mandy's breath stopped in her throat. She could see no sign of life.

Gently she put a hand to the vixen's side. She was still breathing. Mandy could feel the slight rise and fall of her side. But she was getting cold despite her thick coat.

Mandy looked around desperately for something to cover the two animals with – something to keep them warm. There was nothing. Quickly she pulled off her jumper and tucked it round vixen and cub, stroking the vixen's head and murmuring to her.

'It won't be long now,' she said. 'James will be back soon with Mum and then everything will be fine. You'll see. Mum and Dad look after lots of animals at Animal Ark.'

The vixen's dark eyes opened briefly as Mandy spoke. It was as if they were pleading with her for help. Mandy laid a hand on the vixen's pointed muzzle and continued to speak in a soothing, comforting voice. She knew that talking gently to hurt animals helped to calm them. It helped to keep their pulses steady and to reassure them if they were in shock. So she sat by the vixen and her cub and told them all about Welford and Animal Ark and her mother and father, Adam and Emily Hope, who were vets, and Gran and Grandad who lived in the village and James, her best friend, and his Labrador, Blackie.

She was deep in a description of Gran and Grandad's new camper van when she felt the cub squirm under her jumper and make a tiny sound. Mandy smiled in spite of her worry. 'You're a fighter, aren't you?' she said.

Just then there was a sound of a car engine and

the scrape of tyres drawing up. *Mum and James*, Mandy thought, then she hesitated. It could be the person who had set the trap! If it was, she would have to be careful. She bit her lip as she looked down at the two helpless animals. Even if it was the trap setter, the animals would still be safe. Mandy would see to that.

She leaped to her feet and scrambled up the banking. There was a sound of voices and a bright flash of red hair beyond the trees. There was no mistaking Mrs Hope's hair. It glowed like copper. It was Mum and James after all.

'Mum!' she called. 'Over here. Hurry!'

Mrs Hope and James came running through the trees. Mandy thought she had never been so glad to see her mum.

'I was as quick as possible,' said James.

Mandy smiled. 'I know. It just seemed like an age, that's all.'

'Well,' said Mrs Hope, smiling down at Mandy. 'I hear you've rescued a fox this time.' Her green eyes were bright with concern. Looking at them, Mandy felt a terrific sense of relief. It would be all right now that Mum was here.

'And a cub, Mum,' said Mandy, almost pushing her mother down towards the hollow in her eagerness. 'But the vixen is hurt and very weak and the cub is so tiny. You can help them, Mum, can't you?'

Emily Hope looked down at the anxious faces of James and Mandy. 'I can do my best,' she said gently. Then her voice became brisk. 'Now, where are my patients?'

Mandy pointed to her green jumper tucked round the foxes. 'There,' she said and Mrs Hope smiled.

'Is that the new one Gran knitted for you?' she said.

'Gran won't mind,' said Mandy. 'It's in a good cause.'

She felt so much better now that her mum was here with her vet's bag and her gentle hands, kneeling beside the foxes, undoing Mandy's jumper, searching with quick, practised fingers for injury.

Mrs Hope understood how Mandy felt about animals, especially young orphaned animals. She understood because she and Adam Hope had adopted Mandy when Mandy became an orphan. Mandy's real parents had been killed in a car crash when she was a baby but, for her, Adam and Emily Hope were as real as any mum and dad could be. In fact to Mandy they were the best mum and dad in the world.

At last Emily Hope straightened up. Her face was serious and Mandy's heart sank.

'You *can* help, can't you, Mrs Hope?' James said.

Mandy's mum pursed her lips. 'The vixen has lost a lot of blood,' she said. 'She's very weak. The wound in her upper leg is deep. If we move her it might start to bleed again.'

Mandy nodded. 'It *did* start to bleed again when she tried to move.'

Emily Hope nodded. 'It isn't just that, Mandy. It's also the blood she has lost after giving birth. I'm afraid the shock of being caught in the trap brought it on early. Animals in shock are much less likely to survive, you know.'

'Can't you do anything, Mum?' Mandy said.

Emily Hope shook her head. 'Not here,' she said. 'I need clean water for a start.' She looked around the wood. The light filtered dimly through the trees. 'And I need a good light to work in. I'll have to stitch this leg and I think there's a good chance she'll need an operation.'

'Then we'll take them to Animal Ark,' Mandy said.

Mrs Hope didn't say anything for a moment.

'Mum?' said Mandy. 'What's wrong?'

Mrs Hope sighed. 'Mandy,' she said slowly, 'if I move her it might be too much for her. Animal Ark is too far away. I don't think I'd get her there alive.'

Mandy was close to tears. 'What about the cub?' she said. 'Can you save the cub?'

Emily Hope's eyes were sad. 'I'm afraid the cub can't survive without his mother – not for two or three weeks yet.'

'But we have to do something,' said James. 'We can't just leave them to die.'

Mrs Hope nodded. 'I agree,' she said. 'We'll try to get them to Animal Ark. I just wanted you to understand the risks.'

'No,' said Mandy suddenly. 'It's too dangerous.'

James and Mrs Hope looked at her.

'You mean you want to leave them here?' said James as if he couldn't believe his ears.

Mandy shook her head. 'No,' she said. 'I want to take them to The Riddings. It's only five minutes away by car. Could you manage to work there, Mum? Would that do?'

Emily Hope looked doubtful, then she said. 'Yes, I could manage. It's certainly better than trying to take the animals all the way to Animal Ark.'

'What will the Spry sisters say?' said James.

Mandy shrugged. 'We'll see when we get there,'

she said. 'Come on, James. There's no time to lose.'

'There's a sack in the back of the car, Mandy,' Emily Hope said. 'Run and fetch it. We can use it as a stretcher.'

When Mandy got back with the sack she found that her mum had put a tight bandage round the vixen's leg.

'This will stop it bleeding,' said Emily Hope. 'But there's no time to waste. We can't leave that on too long or the leg will be permanently damaged. You can only stop the blood getting to it for so long without risk.'

Mandy spread the sack out and Mrs Hope laid the vixen on top. 'You take one end and I'll take the other, James,' she said. 'And be careful. The vixen is too weak to snap just at the moment. But don't forget, she's a wild animal. Mandy, you can bring the cub.'

Mandy picked up the scrap of life that was the cub. He was so tiny. But he was warm and his little tongue flicked out and rubbed against her hand as she held him. Then she looked down and felt her throat tighten.

'Mum,' she said. 'What about the other cubs, the ones that didn't survive? We can't just leave them here like this.'

Mrs Hope stretched out a hand and laid it on Mandy's shoulder. 'We have to – for the moment,' she said. 'We have to try to save the vixen and her cub. It's a hard lesson to learn, Mandy, but the living come first.'

Mandy felt tears prick behind her eyes. But her mum was right. Even the vixen had wasted no time on the cubs that she couldn't help. Instead she had saved the one who was still alive. It was the instinct of survival.

'Dad will come up later and bury these little ones,' Emily Hope said.

Mandy nodded. She couldn't speak. But she knew that what her mother said made sense even if it was hard to accept.

The little procession made its way up out of the hollow towards the road where Mrs Hope's four-wheel drive waited. James took the back seat with the vixen beside him and Mandy slid into the seat beside her mother, the tiny cub cradled in her arms.

She looked down at the little bundle of fur. At least this one had a chance of surviving – if they could save its mother. 'Oh, please let us be in time,' she whispered. 'Please.'

* * *

The Riddings was a huge old house set back from wide sweeping lawns. As Mrs Hope drove up the driveway towards the massive stone staircase in front of the house Mandy looked at the turrets and battlements. What a place for two elderly ladies to live in!

The Spry sisters were twins. Mandy didn't know how old they were exactly but they looked ancient. They lived at The Riddings all alone except for Geoffrey, the gardener.

Geoffrey was even more ancient than the sisters. He hardly ever set foot inside the house. Then there was Patch, the kitten the Spry sisters had adopted when Mandy and James were looking for homes for four kittens.

'Will they let us in?' said James.

'Of course they will,' said Mandy. 'They took Patch in, didn't they? They wouldn't turn away a wounded animal.'

Mrs Hope brought the four-wheel drive to a stop just as the front door opened. Miss Marjorie Spry peered round the door. 'Have you forgotten something, Mrs Hope?' she said nervously, her hands pulling at the ancient cardigan she wore.

Emily Hope got out of the car and opened the door for James to get out with the vixen. 'No,' she said. 'But we have a wounded fox here and we need your help.'

'Our help?' said another voice and Miss Joan appeared behind her sister.

Mandy held her breath. Then, between the feet of Miss Joan, a little cat appeared.

'Patch!' said Mandy. 'How is he?'

Miss Marjorie smiled. 'Your mother said it was nothing to worry about,' she said. 'Just a little cold. But you can't be too careful, can you?'

Mrs Hope smiled back. 'No, indeed,' she said, and waited while Miss Marjorie and Miss Joan looked at each other and then at James with the vixen in his arms.

'It's so good of you to come and see Patch here,' said Miss Marjorie to Mrs Hope.

'We don't go out much,' finished Miss Joan.

'So I think, since you are always so understanding . . .' said Miss Marjorie.

'. . . we must do all we can for you,' said Miss Joan.

It was amazing how they finished each other's sentences, Mandy thought.

'Come in,' said Miss Marjorie, holding the door wide.

Mandy heaved a sigh of relief and cuddled the cub in her jumper. 'Oh, thank you,' she said. 'Thank you so much.'

'We'd like to use your kitchen,' said Emily Hope. 'And we have no time to lose.' Already she was hurrying into the house, Mandy and James and the twin sisters following her.

The kitchen was vast and old-fashioned. Mandy's mother cleared a space on the kitchen table and laid a polythene sheet from her bag over it. Mandy watched her mother proudly.

At once Emily Hope was businesslike, ordering water to be boiled, unpacking her bag, setting everything out on the kitchen table. At last she was ready.

'Mandy,' she said, 'you'll have to help me. I'm going to stitch the wound in the leg first but she might need some more treatment. We'll have to see. That birth couldn't have been easy for her.'

Mandy nodded and handed the cub to James. Immediately the Spry sisters clustered round.

'Oh, how tiny,' said Miss Marjorie. 'And look at those little ears – all tightly curled up.'

'We must find something to put it in,' said Miss Joan. 'Come with us, young man.'

James set the cub carefully down on the table. It moved slightly, snuggling into Mandy's warm jumper. As he followed the sisters out of the kitchen, James looked back.

'Go on,' said Mandy. 'We'll look after the cub.'

Mandy watched her mum scrub up at the kitchen sink, then put on rubber gloves. She took a spray from her bag and sprayed the vixen's leg.

'A local anaesthetic to freeze the wound is all I dare risk,' she said to Mandy. She pointed to her stethoscope. 'Take that, Mandy, and listen to her breathing for me while I work. If there's any change let me know at once.' She looked down at her patient. 'And if I need you down here I'll tell you.'

Mandy went to the vixen's head and began to stroke it. The vixen's eyes were still closed. She looked very weak and small. Mandy put the stethoscope on. It wasn't the first time she had used one; her dad had shown her how to listen for a heartbeat, how to detect changes in breathing. The vixen's heartbeat seemed steady.

As her mum worked, Mandy listened to the vixen's heart. From time to time she spoke to the animal, gently, calming. Once the fox opened her eyes and Mandy saw the fright in them. She looked over at her mum. Emily Hope was bent over her patient.

'Not long now,' Mandy said to the vixen. 'It'll soon be over.'

'Mandy,' said Emily Hope, 'come and help.'

Mandy took the wad of gauze Mrs Hope was holding out.

'Just dab it as I work,' said Mrs Hope.

Mandy looked at the neat row of stitches her mother had put in the vixen's leg. There was blood at the edges of the wound. Mandy dabbed as her mother put in the last few stitches.

'How is she?' said Mandy.

Her mother shook her head. 'The leg wound should be OK,' she said. 'But I want to get her down to Animal Ark for a thorough investigation. After all, she's just had cubs and she's weak and in shock. She'll need an injection against infection and a lot of tender loving care.'

Mandy smiled. 'I can give her that,' she said.

Mandy's mother smiled back. 'If the vixen pulls through you'll be busy enough looking after her cub,' she said.

Just at that moment James came back into the kitchen with the Spry sisters. He was carrying a cat basket. Inside the basket was a scrap of blue blanket. Gently, he lifted the cub and placed him in the basket on top of the blanket.

'Why, that's perfect for carrying him!' said Emily Hope.

The sisters beamed. 'He's so tiny. James told us what happened, Mandy. Nasty wicked things, gin traps. Father never used them,' Miss Joan said.

'Father used to hunt foxes,' said Miss Marjorie. 'He used to say that at least that way you got a bit of sport.'

'But Father did *not* approve of traps,' Miss Joan said.

Mandy opened her mouth to say that she thought fox-hunting was cruel, then she closed it again. The Spry sisters had been so kind, letting them use their kitchen, providing a basket for the cub – even a blanket to keep him warm.

And the cub and his mother were safe now. That was all that mattered.

Three

The journey to Animal Ark was a lot less worrying than the one to The Riddings had been. At least the vixen had stopped bleeding.

'She isn't out of danger yet, though,' said Emily Hope. 'I'd like to see what Dad says.'

As they drew up to Animal Ark, Adam Hope was coming round the corner of the house from the surgery. He was wearing a track suit; he had taken to jogging to try and get his weight down. His dark hair was tousled from his run.

Mandy looked at the old, stone cottage with the wooden sign that said 'Animal Ark, Veterinary Surgeon' swinging in the breeze. Banks of flowers bordered the path and the stone flags glowed mellow in the sunlight. She loved her home. Already, she felt the fox and cub were safer just because they were here.

'Hi, you lot,' called Adam Hope, coming towards them and smiling his special lop-sided smile. Even his beard couldn't hide that smile. 'What have you got there?'

Mandy opened the cat basket and showed him, while James told the story of finding the vixen.

Mr Hope's eyes darkened as he listened. 'Disgusting things these traps,' he said as he took the vixen from his wife. He began to carry it round to the surgery. 'They're illegal for a start, and dangerous to all kinds of animals.'

'And to children,' said Mrs Hope. 'Can you imagine a small child coming across one of those? It doesn't bear thinking about.'

'Should we tell the police?' James said. 'They could find out who set the trap, couldn't they?'

Mr Hope shook his head. 'Whoever set this isn't going to admit to the police that they did it,' he said. 'And anyway, there could be other traps.'

'You mean more foxes could be getting trapped in these horrible things?' said Mandy. 'Then we *should* tell the police. They could search for them.'

They were at the surgery entrance now and Emily Hope pushed open the door. 'Unless you knew exactly where to look, it would be a waste of time,' she said. 'You could look for weeks and never find it. The police don't have time for that kind of thing. Even if the people who set the traps are caught, they will only get fined. It won't stop them doing it.'

'My goodness, what have you got there?' said a voice from behind the reception desk. Jean Knox, the receptionist, peered at them. She caught hold of the glasses that were dangling from a chain round her neck and put them on. 'Good heavens,' she said as she saw the new patients.

'A fox and her cub, Jean,' said Dad. 'We're just going to give the vixen a thorough check-up now. Mandy and James will settle the cub in the residential unit.' He turned to Mandy. 'Don't forget to put him in the annex,' he said.

Mandy nodded. The annex was a little room at the back of the residential unit. It had recently been set up for the wild animals that sometimes had to be treated at Animal Ark.

'Simon is in the surgery,' Jean said.

Mandy looked at James as her mum and dad disappeared into the surgery. 'The vixen will be

OK,' James said reassuringly.

'I hope so,' said Mandy looking down at the cat basket. The cub was beginning to stir. 'If she doesn't survive, the cub won't either.'

'Come on,' said James. 'Let's get him settled.' And he held open the door to the unit.

Mandy nodded. 'We'll need a cage big enough for both of them,' she said.

'It's a pity they can't be with the other animals,' James said.

Mandy shook her head. 'You know how careful we have to be about cross-infection,' she said. 'Mum and Dad always keep the wild animals separate from the domestic ones.'

They found a large cage and Mandy laid the cub in it, tucking his blanket round him. The little animal barely stirred while she did it.

'He's fast asleep again,' said James.

Mandy sighed. 'I suppose he'll be getting hungry soon,' she said. 'James, what if his mother isn't well enough to feed him?'

James turned from the cage. 'It'll be all right,' he said. 'You'll see. Your mum and dad are terrific vets.' He smiled. 'Tell you what, let's go and visit the other animals.'

Mandy smiled back. 'OK,' she said, 'Let's start with

the cats. But first we'll have to wash our hands after handling the cub.'

James and Mandy made a complete tour of the unit. It was certainly better than just waiting around brooding. As well as the cats, there were a couple of guinea-pigs who snuffled at the bars of their cage as Mandy approached.

'Hello, Tig and Tag,' Mandy said to the guinea-pigs. They were waiting to be collected by their new owner. She popped a couple of carrots into their cage as a treat.

'Poor Jilly,' said James, standing beside a cage with a very sorry-looking puppy in it. 'What's wrong with her?'

'She's just had her injections,' Mandy said, 'and she didn't like them much.'

Jilly woofed softly and came and licked James's hand through the wire of her cage. James gave in. 'OK,' he said, 'Let's give you a cuddle then,' and he lifted the puppy out of the cage and brought her over to Mandy.

Mandy was standing beside a cage with a tortoise in it.

'She's got something wrong with her eye,' Mandy said to James. 'But she's getting better.'

'Of course she is,' said James. 'With your mum

and dad looking after her, she's bound to get better.'

Mandy looked at James standing there holding the puppy. 'And I feel better too,' she said. 'Thanks, James.'

James flushed. 'No problem,' he said. He went to put Jilly back in her cage to hide his embarrassment.

The door to the unit opened and Mr Hope came in.

Mandy held her breath. 'Will the vixen get better?' she said.

Her dad nodded but she could see a line of worry round his mouth.

'There are some complications,' he said. 'Mum thought there would be. The vixen wasn't quite ready to have her cubs. She'll need to stay here for a few weeks. There's no way she's fit to be out in the wild yet.'

'So the cub will be all right?' said Mandy.

Emily Hope came in with Simon behind her carrying the vixen. Mandy and James followed them through to the annex where the foxes' cage was.

'She might have a bit of bother feeding the cub,' said Emily Hope. 'You two will have to help.'

'Oh, we'll do anything. Won't we, James?' said Mandy eagerly.

Mandy's mother laughed. 'Let's see if you say that

when you're in here every few hours trying to top up the cub's feed,' she said.

'We'll take it in turns,' said James, but Mandy didn't mind how often she had to feed the cub. The vixen was going to survive. She and James would look after the cub.

Simon bent down and laid the vixen next to her cub. At once the tiny scrap snuggled up and nuzzled for a feed.

'She doesn't have a lot of milk,' said Emily Hope.

'It's just as well she only has the one cub to feed,' said Adam Hope. He turned to Mandy. 'Mum told me about the other cubs,' he said. 'I'll go up there now and attend to things. You know, Mandy,' he added very gently, 'if she was trying to feed more than one cub she would never manage it. It would put all their lives at risk. She'll have a hard enough job feeding that one.'

'She's so small,' said Mrs Hope, 'but it's lucky for her she is. If her leg hadn't been so slender it would have been smashed in that trap and beyond repair.'

Simon grinned at them all. 'I'd say it was this little fellow that was lucky,' he said, tickling the cub under the chin. 'Lucky that you two came along.'

Mandy smiled down at the mother and baby snuggled up closely together. 'Then that's what we'll call the cub,' she said. 'We'll call him Lucky.'

The next two weeks were incredibly busy for Mandy. Mrs Hope had been right when she said Mandy would have her work cut out for her. The vixen was still weakened by her ordeal, but she was managing to feed Lucky a little each day and Mandy soon learned to top up the cub's diet with warm milk. At first, she had to use a doll's feeding-bottle. Then Lucky grew big enough to manage a baby's feeding-bottle. Then, on the eleventh day, his eyes opened.

'They're blue!' Mandy said to James when he made

his regular afternoon visit to the foxes.

Lucky looked up at the sound of her voice and yawned. Mandy yawned too and James laughed.

'You're tired,' he said.

'It's been hard work,' said Mandy. 'But that doesn't matter.' She stifled another yawn. 'Look, James. I thought his eyes would be brown.'

The cub's blue-grey eyes blinked up at them sleepily before they closed again and he curled up, asleep.

'Aren't you proud of him?' said Mandy to Lucky's mother. The vixen was still very weak. But there was a brightness in her eyes that hadn't been there a week ago. 'Come on,' Mandy said to James. 'Let's tell Mum.'

They found Mrs Hope clearing up after surgery.

'Great news,' she said when they told her. 'Of course his eyes will turn brown in time.' She smiled. 'He's making really good progress. And so is his mother.'

As Lucky grew bigger Mandy began to give him bread soaked in milk and honey. At two weeks he began to take notice of what was going on round about him, and after another week he was eating solid food and exploring his cage. Mandy let him out for a little while each day and soon he was into everything, tumbling round the floor and getting up to mischief.

'He's quite a handful,' Simon said to Mandy one day, as he was doing the medications.

Mandy laughed. She was giving the foxes' cage a thorough clean. Mother and cub were on the floor, Lucky romping around his mother, trying to get her to play with him.

'She still isn't completely better,' said Mandy, looking at the vixen.

Mr Hope came in with a small bundle in his arms. 'I want this puppy to stay overnight just to keep an eye on him,' he said to Simon. He looked at the foxes. 'You know, Mandy, I think it's time to separate Lucky from his mother. She isn't really up to all this romping around. And now that he's on solid food he doesn't need to be near her all the time.'

Mandy nodded. 'That's true. He eats anything,' she said.

Mr Hope laughed. 'That's one thing about foxes,' he said. 'They aren't too fussy about what they eat. Rabbits, hedgehogs, birds – as well as any kitchen scraps they can find.'

Mandy smiled. 'Lucky likes honey and sponge cake best,' she said.

'I hope that isn't all you give him,' Mr Hope said.

'Oh, no,' said Mandy. 'He can manage stewed apples and minced beef and all kinds of things.'

'I'm glad to hear it,' Mr Hope said. 'But I'd like his mother's appetite to improve. She's still far from well.'

Mandy bit her lip. 'Maybe Lucky tires her too much,' she said. 'Should I put him in a separate cage?'

Mr Hope smiled. 'If he'll stay there,' he said. 'Foxes are very good at getting out of things like cages. But you can try.'

Mandy grinned. 'He's adorable, isn't he?' she said.

'Adorable,' said her dad as Lucky loped over to him and started trying to nip his ankle.

There was a voice outside and the sound of bicycle wheels on gravel. Mandy turned. 'That's James,' she said. 'We're going on a bike ride.'

'Put Lucky back first,' said Mr Hope. 'If you can catch him.'

Lucky was scampering across the floor. Occasionally he would overbalance and roll over. 'I can catch him. I can run faster than he can,' said Mandy.

Her dad grinned back. 'Give him a couple of weeks,' he said, 'and then watch him run. That little fellow is going to be a holy terror.'

She scooped Lucky up off the floor and put him and his mother back in their cage.

Mr Hope reached for another cage. 'Put the cub in here. Give the poor vixen a bit of a rest.' He paused. 'There's another reason,' he said.

Mandy looked at him. 'What?' she said.

'Well,' said Mr Hope. 'The vixen is getting a bit better now. She notices what's going on around her. I don't want her to get too used to us. You see, if she loses her fear of human beings she might have trouble surviving in the wild.'

'You mean I have to stay away from her?' Mandy said.

'It's hard, I know,' said Mr Hope. 'But the less she's fussed over, the better it will be for her in the end. After all, when we release her, she has to teach Lucky to look after himself. And she can't do that if she trusts humans too much.'

Mandy frowned. 'But we would never hurt them,' she said.

'No,' said Mr Hope slowly. 'But other people might. Remember the trap?'

Mandy frowned. 'Does that mean I can't look after Lucky either?' she said.

'No,' said Mr Hope. 'He's young and he'll learn from his mother once we release him. But you can't make a pet of him. It wouldn't be fair.'

Mandy transferred the cub and his blanket to the cage her dad was holding open. Lucky was very fond of his blanket. She snapped down the latch and looked at the cub. She would miss him when he was gone. But he was a wild animal and Mandy knew that Dad was right.

James came in just as Mandy finished washing her hands. He had Blackie with him. The Labrador's tail was wagging so hard it looked as if it was about to fly off.

'Hello, Blackie,' Mandy said getting down on her knees and putting her arms round the dog's neck.

Blackie licked her face and wagged his tail even more.

Mandy looked at James. 'Let's forget the bike ride and take Blackie for a good long walk,' she said.

James nodded. 'That's just what Mum suggested when he knocked over her favourite vase and broke it. You don't mind, do you?'

Mandy grinned. Blackie was the friendliest dog in the world but he was also accident-prone and disobedient.

At that moment her mother came into the unit. 'Emergency,' she said to Mr Hope. 'There's a cow calving up at Twyford and it's in trouble. I have to

go.' She looked at Mandy. 'I've got some medicine
for Patch,' she said. 'Would you deliver it for me? I
promised the Sprys I'd get it to them this afternoon.'

Mandy nodded eagerly. 'I've been wanting to go
and thank them for what they did for the foxes,' she
said. 'Of course we'll go, won't we, James?'

James nodded. 'Sure,' he said. 'Blackie can still
get his walk. If we don't go too fast he can run along
beside us. He loves doing that.'

Mandy's mum handed her a small bottle of
eardrops. 'It's his ears again,' she said. 'Tell the sisters
not to worry. One drop in each ear morning and
night and Patch will be as fit as a fiddle in a few
days.'

'I'll tell them,' said Mandy as she put the bottle in
her pocket. Then she turned to James. 'Race you,'
she said and she was out of the door and on her
bike before he had time to reply.

James caught up with her at the corner by the Fox
and Goose. They pedalled peacefully along together,
not going too fast for Blackie's sake. The Labrador
was having a wonderful time investigating the
hedgerows and ditches and loping off over the wall
that bordered the road. Mandy could see his black,
plumy tail waving above the long grass of Redpath's
field as they came round by the church. James

whistled and Blackie gave an answering bark, but he didn't come to heel.

'That dog *never* listens,' Mandy laughed.

James shook his head ruefully. 'Don't I know it!' he said. 'I just wish I could persuade Mum it's not worth trying. She thinks I should take him to obedience classes!'

'What obedience classes?' said Mandy.

James looked miserable. 'Mrs Ponsonby's,' he said. 'She's advertising them at the village hall. Mum heard about it when she was at the WI last week.'

Mandy gaped. Mrs Ponsonby was a very large, very determined woman who liked to think she ran the whole village. She had blue-rinsed hair and pink spectacles and a voice like a foghorn. She also had two dogs, a Pekinese called Pandora and a mongrel called Toby.

'I suppose she's all right really,' Mandy said. 'I mean she took Toby in when he had no home.' Mandy thought of the poor abandoned little puppy. 'But I still wouldn't want to go to her obedience classes,' she said. 'And anyway Blackie's just – well, Blackie,' she finished and grinned at James.

'That's just it,' said James. 'I like Blackie just the way he is. I don't want anybody to change him.'

Mandy lifted her head. 'In that case,' she said,

'we've got to make sure Blackie doesn't go to those obedience classes.'

'How are we going to do that?' said James.

Mandy shrugged. 'Something will turn up,' she said. 'It's bound to. I mean, can you imagine that dog *ever* listening to you?'

Four

When they got to The Riddings there was a car drawn up in front of the house. Mandy recognised the driver.

'It's Dennis Saville,' she said to James.

James grimaced. Dennis Saville worked for Sam Western, who owned the most modern farm in the district. Neither Mandy nor James liked Dennis Saville or Sam Western. In fact, they had good cause to dislike them quite a lot after the two men had tried to poison a goat belonging to a friend of theirs.

'He's got the dogs with him,' James said as Dennis Saville got out of the car and opened the back door to let two bulldogs out.

Mandy looked at the powerful dogs. She loved all animals but these dogs had been trained to be suspicious and unfriendly. It wasn't the dogs' fault. It was their owner's.

Blackie came loping out of the trees that grew almost up to the driveway and the two bulldogs growled.

'Here, Blackie,' James said quickly.

Blackie didn't stop. He trotted up to the two bulldogs, his tongue hanging out, grinning in a friendly fashion.

The bulldogs snarled and Dennis Saville caught their collars.

'Call your dog!' he said sharply to James.

James got off his bike and went and grabbed Blackie's collar. He clipped on the lead and almost had to drag him away from the other two dogs. Blackie seemed to be wondering why he couldn't have a nice game with the bulldogs.

'Keep him tied up,' said Dennis Saville, shortly. 'If you know what's good for him, that is!' And he strode off down the drive with the bulldogs at his heels.

'What a cheek,' said Mandy. 'You'd think he owned the place.'

She stroked Blackie. 'Poor Blackie; you're so friendly, aren't you?'

James was red with embarrassment and annoyance. 'Maybe Mum's right,' he said. 'Maybe Blackie does need obedience classes.'

Mandy's mouth set firmly. 'I like him just as he is,' she said. 'Let's deliver those eardrops and get out of here.'

It was Miss Marjorie who opened the door.

'We've brought Patch's eardrops,' said Mandy. 'Mum says he'll be fine in a day or two and not to worry.'

But Miss Marjorie looked very worried indeed. She took the eardrops gratefully. 'That was kind of you,' she said. But Mandy could tell her mind was on something else.

'Is anything wrong, Miss Marjorie?' she asked.

Miss Marjorie put her hand to her head. 'It's so confusing,' she said, 'and I'm sure we don't want to be spoilsports, but really we don't know what to tell him.'

'Who?' said Mandy.

'Why, Mr Western of course,' said Miss Marjorie. 'He's with Joan now.'

Mandy looked at her. 'What does Mr Western want?' she said.

Miss Marjorie looked surprised. 'Why, he wants to start a fox-hunt,' she said. 'Didn't I say? But, of course, he needs our permission to hunt over our land.'

Mandy was horrified. 'You won't let him, will you, Miss Marjorie?' she said.

Miss Marjorie looked doubtful. 'Dear Papa always used to hunt,' she said.

'But it's wrong,' said Mandy. 'Fox-hunting is cruel.'

James caught her arm as a figure emerged from the dining-room. He had grey-blond hair combed carefully into a quiff and he wore very smart tweeds. 'I shall expect your answer very soon, Miss Joan,' he was saying to the other twin.

Miss Joan fluttered her hands. 'Really, Mr Western, I don't know,' she was saying.

Sam Western turned to her. 'Just think what your father would say,' he said. '*He* wouldn't have any doubts.'

Miss Joan fluttered her hands again. 'But neither Marjorie nor I ever liked fox-hunting,' she said.

Me Western looked down at her sternly. 'Your father would be ashamed of you,' he said. And he turned and marched straight past Mandy and James, hardly looking at them.

Mandy watched as he strode out of the door. She

turned to Miss Joan. 'You can't let him do it,' she said. 'It's so cruel.'

'Oh, dear,' said Miss Joan. 'Marjorie, whatever are we to do?'

Mandy looked at the sisters. 'Just tell him,' she said. 'Tell him he can't hunt on your land.'

Miss Marjorie pursed her lips. 'How can we?' she said. 'He isn't the sort of person you can "just tell".'

Mandy frowned. Miss Marjorie was right. Sam Western wasn't the type to listen to something he didn't want to hear and the sisters were far too timid to deal with him.

There was only one thing to do. She grabbed

James's arm. 'We've got to go now,' she said to the sisters, as she hurried James out of the door. 'Give our love to Patch.'

'Where are we going in such a rush?' said James.

Mandy's face was grim. 'If the sisters can't persuade him it's wrong then we have to,' she said.

'Mr Western?' said James. 'I don't fancy our chances.'

But Mandy wasn't listening. They had reached the bottom of the steps and Sam Western was just getting into his car. Dennis Saville was holding the car door open for him. The dogs were already in the back. Mr Western was speaking to Dennis Saville, his voice quite clear. Mandy shrank back behind the stone balustrade and pulled James with her. 'Listen,' she whispered.

'And if I lay my hands on whoever sprang that trap they'll be sorry, believe me,' he was saying.

Dennis Saville nodded. 'At least the other one is untouched,' he said. 'Why on earth would anybody bother with them? Foxes are nothing but vermin.'

Mandy felt her face go white. She grasped James's arm as Mr Western got into the car and drove away.

'Did you hear that?' she said to James. 'They're the ones who set that trap! *And* they've laid another one!'

'You'll never persuade him to give up this idea of fox-hunting,' James said. 'Did you hear what he said about foxes being vermin?'

Mandy nodded. She thought of Lucky and his mother. How could anybody call them vermin? How could anybody lay such cruel traps for animals? She turned to James, her face determined.

'There's nothing we can do,' said James before she could speak. 'Except maybe try and make the Spry sisters stand up to him.'

Mandy nodded again. 'We can try that,' she said. 'But there's something else we have to do first.'

'What's that?' said James.

'We have to find that other trap before some other poor animal is caught in it.'

James shook his head slowly. 'That won't be easy,' he said. 'It could be anywhere. Remember what your dad said.'

'I know,' said Mandy, 'but we've got to try, James. Just think if another animal got caught. We might not be there to rescue it.'

James was looking at the powerful car as it swept down the drive and out through the gates. 'OK,' he said. 'We'll try. And if anybody can do it we can.'

Mandy's face was determined. 'We'll beat him yet,' she said. 'Just see if we don't.'

* * *

But when they got back to Animal Ark they found they had another problem on their hands.

Mandy looked round the residential unit. Bedding was strewn across the floor, a couple of feeding dishes were overturned and Lucky was nowhere to be seen.

'Where is he?' she said to Jean, who was in the middle of clearing up.

Jean shook her head. 'Disappeared,' she said.

'But how did he get out?' said Mandy. 'I fastened the cage. I know I did.'

Mr Hope turned from where he was renewing a dressing on a kitten's leg. 'They don't talk about being cunning as a fox for nothing, Mandy,' he said. 'My guess is he slipped the latch on his cage. He's a clever little thing.'

Mandy breathed a sigh of relief. 'You aren't angry then?' she said.

Mr Hope grinned. 'There isn't any point in being angry,' he said. 'It's in a fox cub's nature to be mischievous, and his mother isn't well enough yet to keep him in line.'

Mandy looked at the vixen. She was lying peacefully in her cage. Her leg was mending well enough but her coat was dull and she was very thin. 'We'll find Lucky, Dad.'

'But where?' said James.

Mr Hope laughed. 'Don't worry too much about that,' he said. 'Lucky is still too young to want to go too far away from his mother. But in a week or so . . .'.

'What?' said Mandy.

Mr Hope put the kitten back in his cage and came over to them. 'It's the other animals I'm worried about,' he said. 'If Lucky can open his own cage he can open others. Some of the animals are still pretty ill. There's also the risk of cross-infection. We can't let wild animals come into close contact with domestic animals.'

Mandy's heart was sinking. 'But the vixen isn't well enough to be released into the wild yet,' she said. 'You said it would be another two weeks at least.'

Mr Hope nodded. 'That's true,' he said. 'But Lucky is already on solid food. In a week or so he should be weaned completely. That will be good for his mother. She can use all her strength to get better.'

'And Lucky?' said Mandy. 'You can't let Lucky go all on his own. He's far too little.'

Mr Hope shook his head. 'I wasn't thinking that,' he said. 'But I don't think he can stay here.'

'So where is he to go?' said Mandy.

Mr Hope smiled gently. 'I think that's up to you

and James,' he said. 'You'll have to find another home for him until he and his mother can be released together. I'm sorry, Mandy, but it has to be. Once Lucky's got a taste for freedom there will be no holding him. You must see I can't risk the welfare of the other animals.'

Mandy nodded miserably. Where were they going to find another home for Lucky? If he caused trouble at Animal Ark he would cause trouble anywhere.

'Meanwhile . . .' Mr Hope began.

'Yes?' said Mandy.

Her dad grinned. 'Don't you think you'd better go and see if you can find him?'

'Cripes,' said James and Mandy gasped.

'Where shall we start?' she said, looking at James.

James looked just as lost as she felt. One way and another the problems just seemed to be piling up. First the fox-hunting, then the other trap and now losing Lucky. Life was very complicated!

They found him at last in the pantry. Emily Hope was holding him gently and scolding him – but not too harshly. 'Is this what you're looking for?' she said, her green eyes dancing.

Mandy nodded, gathering the naughty fox cub into her arms. 'Dad says we have to find another home for him,' she said.

Mrs Hope pursed her lips. 'It might not be a bad idea,' she said. 'Just until they're both fit to be let go. If he stays here, he's in danger of turning into a family pet. That isn't a good idea for a wild animal.'

Mandy nodded. 'That's what Dad says,' she said. 'But where can he go? Who would take him?'

Mrs Hope shook her head. 'You'd need somebody patient, who likes animals, doesn't mind a mess around the place and doesn't mind feeding him regularly.' She sniffed and laughed and said, 'And doesn't mind giving him the occasional bath – which is what I think you two had better do now.'

Mandy looked at her hands. 'Where has he been?' she said.

Emily Hope laughed. 'Oh, in the butter, in the jam, and he managed to knock a bag of sugar over himself.'

James grinned. 'I'll get a basin of water and some soap.'

'And I'll just go and help Dad with the dressings,' said Mrs Hope. 'Something tells me Lucky isn't going to like being bathed very much.'

Mandy held the cub up and looked at him severely.

'Now how are we going to find a home for you if you're so naughty?' she said.

The little cub yawned and tried to nip her finger.

'Rascal,' said Mandy as James came back with a basin full of soapy water and an apron for each of them. 'Just see what happens when you get into such a state!'

Mandy and James were soaked by the time they had finished.

'Gosh, for such a tiny little thing, he's a handful, isn't he?' said James as Lucky splashed water all over him again.

And that was the trouble, Mandy thought. Who on earth could they ask to take on a load of mischief like Lucky?

Five

Mandy and James tried everyone they could think of. But by the middle of the week they still hadn't found a home for Lucky. Either people had enough animals of their own to look after or they were a bit wary of taking in a fox cub. Meanwhile, Lucky was getting even more mischievous as the days went on.

'He got out again this morning,' said Mandy when she met James at the crossroads by the Fox and Goose on Saturday.

'What did he do this time?' said James.

Mandy smiled in spite of herself. 'He got into the flour bin,' Mandy said. 'He seems to like the pantry.'

'I wonder why,' said James, grinning. 'Have you seen this?'

Mandy looked. James was pointing to a poster on the front door of the pub. 'GRAND AUCTION' it said. 'In aid of Cub Scout Funds.'

'I heard about that,' said Mandy. 'The Cub Scouts want to buy tents. I must remember to donate something to it.'

'That's what I like to hear,' said a voice. 'Tommy has his heart set on going to Cub camp this summer.'

Mandy turned to see an old man in a flat cloth cap. It was Walter Pickard. He and Grandad were church bell-ringers together. Walter lived in one of a row of cottages behind the Fox and Goose. Tommy was his great-grandson.

'I hear you've got a fox cub and vixen up at Animal Ark,' the old man went on.

'Oh, Mr Pickard, I don't suppose you could take Lucky in just for a week or so until his mother gets better.'

'Lucky?' said Walter.

Mandy nodded. 'The fox cub. He's getting into mischief and Dad is a bit worried about the other animals.'

Walter shook his head. 'I'd like to help you, young miss,' he said gently. 'But I don't think Tom and

Missie and Scraps would like it.'

Mandy's heart sank. Walter had three cats. Certainly they wouldn't appreciate sharing their home with a fox cub.

'What about your gran and grandad?' said Walter.

'Are they home yet?' said James. 'We thought they were still away.'

'I saw the camper van turning into the lane as I was passing,' said Walter. 'I'm glad to see your grandad back. We've a lot to do to get the auction set up and things collected.'

Mandy and James were already on their bikes, flying towards Lilac Cottage. 'Thanks, Mr Pickard!' Mandy called back.

'Tell your grandad there's bell-ringing practice this afternoon!' Walter called after them. 'I'll see him there!'

Lilac Cottage stood at the end of a lane at the other end of the village. Mandy's grandparents were unloading the camper van as Mandy and James arrived.

'Hi, Gran,' Mandy called, jumping off her bike and throwing herself into her grandmother's arms. Gran hugged her.

'Mandy!' she said breathlessly, 'You'd think we'd been away for a year instead of just two weeks!'

Mandy laughed up into Gran's face. 'You're home early,' she said. 'We thought you were going to be away for longer.'

Gran smiled. 'I got a sudden notion for spring-cleaning,' she said.

Mandy's grandad came out of Lilac Cottage. 'And you know what *that* means,' he said. 'Everything will be topsy-turvy for a week. But once your gran gets a notion for spring-cleaning there's no holding her.'

Gran's eyes twinkled. 'And I saw a lovely three-piece suite in York when we stopped off for lunch,' she said.

Grandad laughed. 'She didn't just see it. It's being delivered on Thursday,' he said. 'And a new china cabinet.'

Gran tutted. 'We need a new china cabinet,' she said. 'That old one is on its last legs.'

'So am I,' joked Grandad. 'Are you going to get a new one of me?'

Mandy laughed. 'Oh, Grandad,' she said. 'There could only ever be one of you.'

Grandad winked at her and Mandy smiled.

Gran tutted. 'Last legs indeed,' she said to Grandad. 'You're as fit as a fiddle.'

'You're only saying that because you want me to

help with your spring-cleaning,' Grandad said to Gran.

Mandy shook her head. It was good to have them home again.

'We've got to get the house in apple pie order for the new furniture,' said Gran.

James looked at Mandy hopelessly and Mandy's face fell as she saw what he was thinking. With spring-cleaning going on and new furniture, Gran wouldn't want a mischievous fox cub running around.

'Lost a pound and found a penny?' Grandad said to her when he saw her glum face.

Mandy explained their problem. Grandad shook his head. 'A fox cub?' he said. 'That's a hard one all right. I don't see many people taking on a bundle of trouble like that.'

'Cubs,' said Gran suddenly. 'That reminds me. Young Tommy Pickard was telling me the Cubs are having a fund-raising auction at the village hall next week.' She looked at Grandad. 'I'll give them the old suite,' she said. 'There's a few good years left in it yet.'

Grandad winked at Mandy. 'That isn't what she said in the shop,' he said.

Mandy laughed. 'Even if you can't take the cub it's still good to have you home,' she said. 'Oh, and

Walter Pickard says he's glad you're home as well –
to help with the auction. And you have bell-ringing
practice this afternoon,' she added.

'At this rate I'll need another holiday,' Grandad
said. But Mandy could see he was still concerned
about her problem. 'Let's go inside and talk about
what you're going to do with this cub,' he said.

'I'll put the kettle on,' said Gran. 'A cup of tea
always makes you feel better. You'll find somebody
to help, Mandy. You've never failed yet.'

'Oh, and another thing, Grandad,' Mandy said as
they all trooped into the cottage. 'Mr Western has
been setting traps for foxes.'

Her grandad looked at her serious face. 'What?'
he said. 'Maybe you'd better tell us all about this.'

Mandy and James told their story over a cup of
tea in the kitchen. 'So you see,' Mandy finished. 'If
the Sprys let him, he'll start fox-hunting. Meantime,
he's setting traps.'

'The Sprys are such gentle people,' said Gran.
'They wouldn't want anything to do with fox-
hunting.'

'They said their father loved hunting,' said James.
'Mr Western has really got at them. He says their
father would be ashamed of them if they didn't let
him use their land .'

'Stuff and nonsense!' said Gran, pouring another cup of tea all round.

Grandad shook his head. 'I remember old Major Spry,' he said. 'He had those girls under his thumb. Sam Western's playing a clever game there.' He looked serious. 'The thing is, I don't like this idea of traps. Anything could get caught in them.'

'That's what *we* thought,' said Mandy. 'We've been looking for the other one but it's like looking for a needle in a haystack!'

Grandad smiled. 'First look for the kind of place you'd find foxes,' he said. 'I don't hold much for Dennis Saville and his like, but he knows his job. He won't have set those traps just anywhere.'

'Where would you look?' said Mandy.

Grandad rubbed his chin. 'Not up on the moors,' he said, 'nor on farmland. They'd be in woodland most probably.'

James nodded. 'That's where the last one was. In Monkton Spinney,' he said.

Grandad nodded. 'That's where I'd look,' he said. Then his face grew serious. 'But if you do find it, stay well away. Don't try anything silly. You could have been badly hurt instead of just getting a scrape, Mandy.'

'That's right,' said Gran. 'You stay well away from

it and report back. Grandad and Walter will see to it.'

Mandy nodded obediently but she couldn't help wondering what would have happened to Lucky if she and James had stayed away from the last trap. The telephone rang then and Gran went to answer it while Grandad and Mandy and James talked over their problem. When she came back Gran was frowning. 'That's a pest,' she said.

'What?' said Mandy.

'Amelia Ponsonby has written out a list of stuff to be donated for the auction,' Gran said. 'She wants somebody to go over to Bleakfell Hall and collect it.'

'What's wrong with giving you the list over the phone?' said Grandad.

Gran grinned. 'She also has a list of suggestions about how the auction should be run,' she said. 'And I wanted to make a start on my spring-cleaning.'

'We'll go,' said Mandy. 'Won't we, James?'

James made a face. Mrs Ponsonby terrified him. She was like a bulldozer. She just flattened everything in her way if she couldn't get what she wanted.

'OK,' said James, not too happily. Then he grinned. 'Do you think she'd take Lucky? She could give him obedience classes!'

Mandy laughed. 'No way,' she said. 'I feel the same way about Lucky as you do about Blackie. I like him just the way he is!'

Bleakfell Hall was a big Victorian mansion. It looked like something out of a horror film with its long driveway and the dense trees around it. In fact, the house had been used not so long ago as a film location by a film company.

They were almost halfway down the drive of the Hall when they heard the commotion. It sounded like two dogs barking and yelping.

'What on earth is that?' said James.

Mandy brought her bike to a halt and listened. There was a high-pitched yapping sound followed by a series of low growls. 'It sounds like Pandora,' she said.

'She sounds frightened,' said James.

'And angry,' said Mandy.

Pandora was Mrs Ponsonby's peke. Mrs Ponsonby and Pandora had been together long before she took on Toby.

'If something happens to Pandora Mrs Ponsonby will—' Mandy stopped. She couldn't imagine *what* Mrs Ponsonby would do. She might be a real dragon at times but she adored her dogs.

'Let's go!' said James.

They leaped off their bikes and plunged into the belt of trees that bordered the driveway.

'Over here!' James shouted as the yapping got more and more frenzied.

Mandy bounded after James and almost cannoned into him when he suddenly stopped.

'What is it?' said Mandy. She looked at the scene in front of her. Pandora was yapping and nipping at Toby, who was crouched in front of her. Toby was circling Pandora, growling fiercely and taking little runs at her, stopping her getting past him.

'Toby!' Mandy shouted.

Toby turned and Pandora took her chance to dash forward. At once Toby was on her, snarling, forcing her back.

Mandy looked at James. 'What on earth is going on?' she said. 'I've never seen Toby behave like this before!'

James shrugged. 'I don't know,' he said. 'But we've got to stop it.'

There was the sound of a voice from the driveway. 'Pandora! Toby!' it called. But neither dog paid attention.

'Mrs Ponsonby,' said Mandy. 'Quick, James. You get Pandora. I'll get Toby.'

They each made a dive for the dogs. Mandy held on to Toby's collar and James scooped Pandora up into his arms where she struggled to get free. Toby continued to bark. They were standing there with the struggling dogs when Mrs Ponsonby appeared through the trees behind them.

She looked at them through her pink spectacles, her blue-rinsed hair quivering with rage as she saw they were holding her precious pets. 'What on earth do you children think you're doing?' she said in a voice like thunder. 'Put my dogs down at once!'

Mandy and James looked at each other. 'Mrs Ponsonby,' said Mandy, 'you're not going to believe this. Toby was attacking Pandora!'

Mrs Ponsonby's face grew so red she looked as if she was going to burst a blood vessel. 'Toby?' she said. 'Attacking my precious Pandora? What nonsense! How dare you speak of Toby like that? I never heard anything so ridiculous in my life.'

'James,' said Mandy. '*James!*' She felt she needed a bit of support here.

But James was looking the other way. 'There's something over there,' he said.

'Where?' said Mandy.

James nodded to where Toby had been. Mandy frowned. 'What on earth was he up to?' she said.

Then, without further ado she thrust Toby into Mrs Ponsonby's arms and walked over to where he had been making such a fuss. Treading carefully through the long grass beneath the trees she looked down – and gasped. 'It's the trap, James!' she said. 'It's the other trap!'

'What trap?' said Mrs Ponsonby. 'What are you talking about? There are no traps on my land.'

James looked at her. 'Dennis Saville put it there,' he said. 'On Mr Western's orders. To catch foxes.'

For once in her life Mrs Ponsonby was speechless. Then she said. 'On *my* land? That man dared to put a trap on *my* land?'

Mandy heaved a sigh of relief. It was clear Mrs Ponsonby knew nothing about it. 'Toby must have been trying to stop Pandora getting near it,' she said. 'You know how nosy Pandora is.'

Mrs Ponsonby drew herself up. 'Inquisitive,' she said.

Mandy smiled. It was one thing Pandora and Mrs Ponsonby had in common – nosiness.

'Anyway I reckon Toby saved Pandora from getting caught in that trap,' said James.

Mrs Ponsonby looked down at Toby. 'My brave boy,' she said. 'What a clever Toby!'

'The question is what are we going to do about it?' said Mandy.

James was still holding Pandora. The little peke was squirming in his arms, still determined to investigate this strange object. 'Your grandad said to leave it alone and let him know,' he said.

Mandy looked at Pandora. 'She'll be over there if we let her go,' she said. 'No, we've got to do something.' She looked around. There were fallen branches lying under the trees. She picked up the heaviest one she could find.

'What are you going to do?' said James.

Mandy's mouth set. 'Spring it,' she said. 'We can't risk leaving it.'

'Be careful,' James said and Mrs Ponsonby echoed his words. Suddenly her face was crumpled with worry. She didn't look her usual confident self.

Slowly, gently, Mandy approached the trap. Its razor sharp jaws gaped at her. She took the branch in both hands and thrust it between the teeth of the trap. At once there was the sound of tearing grass and the clash of steel as the powerful jaws sprang together, almost cutting the heavy branch in two. Mandy felt the judder of the impact in her arms as the trap snatched the branch from her hands. Then she stood back. 'You can let them go now,' she said. 'It's quite safe.'

'My dear child,' said Mrs Ponsonby. 'You're as white as a sheet.'

Mandy let out a deep breath. 'I'm all right,' she said. 'It's Toby who was the hero.'

Mrs Ponsonby's face was grim. 'When I think of what could have happened to my precious Pandora,' she said. 'I'd like to put that man in a trap! I'd like to put him in a cage. In fact I think I'll ask Ernie Bell to make one specially for him. The nerve of it. Putting a trap on *my* grounds!'

Mandy's face brightened. Ernie Bell. She hadn't thought of Ernie Bell. She looked at James and saw the same thought dawn in his mind.

'Do you think he would do it?' he said.

Mandy grinned. 'He might,' she said. 'He took in that squirrel and if anybody can make a cage that will keep Lucky in, he can. It's worth a try, James.'

Mrs Ponsonby looked from one to the other. 'I've no idea what you two are talking about,' she said. 'You're talking in riddles. You must have got a bigger fright than I thought, Mandy. You'd better come up to the house and have a cup of camomile tea. Then you can tell me what's going on – and get that list for your grandmother.' And she turned and marched away, the dogs at her heels.

Mandy and James grinned at each other. Mrs Ponsonby was back to her old self!

Six

Ernie Bell lived in a little cottage a few doors down from Walter Pickard, behind the Fox and Goose pub. Mandy and James wasted no time in getting there.

'We'll have to be careful how we ask,' said Mandy as they parked their bikes outside his cottage.

Ernie's cottage was a picture of neatness. The flower borders marched in a regimented row up the path to the open front door, the windows sparkled like mirrors and the brass handle and letterbox on the shiny dark green front door glittered like gold in the sun. The front door was propped open with a white, painted stone and the doorstep itself gleamed white as new snow in the sunshine.

'Gosh!' said James. 'When did that happen? Ernie's cottage used to look as if it was going to fall down any minute.'

Mandy giggled. 'Mrs Ponsonby told Ernie she didn't think he could look after himself properly and promised to get him a home help.'

'So Ernie cleaned the cottage up?' said James.

Mandy nodded. 'The very next day he was out with the paint pot and the garden tools. Gran says he told her he would show Mrs Ponsonby a thing or two about looking after the place.'

There was a cat sleeping on the doorstep as they approached the door. It woke up and stretched as it heard them.

'Hello, Tiddles,' said Mandy as she bent to stroke the cat. 'I hope your owner is in a good mood today!'

'It won't be easy to get him to agree,' said James thoughtfully. 'But if anybody can build a cage for Lucky, Ernie can. After all, he used to be a carpenter. And he knows how to look after wild animals. He wouldn't make a pet of Lucky. Look at the run he made for Sammy.'

Sammy was an orphaned squirrel Ernie had rescued. He had made a terrific run for the little animal in his back garden. Underneath his crusty exterior Ernie really did have a heart of gold.

Mandy smiled. 'You know how awkward Ernie can be,' she said.

James nodded. 'Like cleaning the cottage up because Mrs Ponsonby thought he couldn't take care of it?'

'So,' said Mandy, 'we've got to make him think he can't do it. Then he'll want to.'

James grinned. 'We've done that before.'

'And it usually works,' said Mandy.

At that moment a small man with short white hair came round the side of the cottage.

'Just go along with anything I say,' Mandy whispered as Ernie saw them.

'Well, you two,' he said. 'And what are you up to now?'

Mandy smiled. 'Hello, Mr Bell. We weren't up to anything. We thought we'd like to see Sammy if that's all right with you.'

Ernie looked at them a bit suspiciously but he couldn't resist a request to see his squirrel. 'Come round the back then,' he said. 'But don't you go feeding him a lot of nonsense now. Young Tommy Pickard was round here yesterday trying to give him biscuits. I don't hold with that. Animals have to keep to their natural foods.'

Mandy thought of Lucky in the pantry but she said, 'Oh, you're right, Mr Bell. It's really important, especially with a wild animal like Sammy.' She looked at James.

'We didn't come just to see Sammy. We wanted to ask your advice as well, Mr Bell,' James said. 'We've got a bit of a problem with a wild animal at the moment.'

Mandy giggled. James made Lucky sound like a man-eating tiger.

'Oh, you have, have you?' said Ernie Bell. 'And what would that be?'

'It's a fox cub, Mr Bell,' Mandy said. 'James and I rescued him and his mother from a trap.'

Ernie Bell looked shocked. 'Don't hold with no traps,' he said. 'Nasty things!'

So far so good, Mandy thought.

They were in Ernie's back garden by this time and James and Mandy stook looking at the run Ernie had made. Sammy the squirrel was scampering to and fro, his eyes bright with curiosity at his visitors.

'Isn't he lovely?' said Mandy, going over to stand by the run.

Sammy scampered up the wire towards her and perched on one of the supports, his paws poised, ready for anything she might offer him.

'I haven't got anything for you, Sammy,' Mandy said and she thought the little squirrel looked disappointed.

'So, what's this about a fox cub, then?' said Ernie.

'Poor little thing,' she said. 'He was only just born when we rescued him. But he's coming along fine now. That's part of the trouble.'

'Trouble?' said Ernie Bell.

Mandy sighed and nodded. 'He keeps escaping from his cage,' she said. 'He gets into everything and he's beginning to upset some of the other animals.'

Ernie had bent to feed Sammy a few nuts.

'Don't tell him that,' James said to Mandy in a whisper. 'You'll put him off.'

Mandy just grinned. 'Trust me,' she said. 'You know how stubborn Ernie is.'

'What's that?' said the old man.

Mandy jumped. 'You've made such a lovely run for Sammy,' said Mandy. 'We thought if we had a look at it we might be able to do the same for Lucky.' She looked critically at the neat dovetail joints and the netting. 'Of course we couldn't hope to do just as well as you.'

James backed her up. 'Not with you being such a

good carpenter,' he said. 'And knowing how to look after wild animals.'

Ernie laid a hand proudly on the fencing of the run. 'It takes years to learn to make dovetail joints as good as that,' he said.

Mandy sighed, 'I know, Mr Bell,' she said. 'But we've got to try. Lucky is so good at escaping we're afraid we're going to lose him altogether. Dad has said we either have to make him secure or find somewhere else for him to go.'

She held her breath, then took the plunge. This was it. If Ernie didn't fall for this they were wasting their time. 'Of course,' she said carefully, 'I don't suppose anybody could make a run that would keep Lucky in, not even you.'

James looked at her. She could see that he was holding his breath as well.

Ernie straightened up slowly and looked at the two of them. 'I don't know about that,' he said. 'I reckon I'm still as good a carpenter as you'll find in Yorkshire.'

'Oh, we didn't mean you weren't,' said James. 'It's just that it would be such a difficult job.' He turned to Mandy. 'But we've got to try, haven't we, Mandy?'

'Before we lose Lucky,' said Mandy.

'And your dad says he can't stay at Animal Ark?' said Ernie.

'It's the other animals,' said Mandy.

Ernie Bell scratched his chin.

'So if you could just give us a drawing we could try and copy it,' said James.

Ernie was still scratching his chin.

'We know it's difficult,' said Mandy.

'Oh, I don't know,' said James, entering into the spirit of the thing. 'It can't be that difficult, can it? I mean all we have to do is make a really strong box – with airholes in it of course.'

Mandy looked at him in horror before she realised what he was up to.

'I suppose so,' she said slowly. 'It wouldn't be too comfortable for him. I mean, he wouldn't have the kind of home Sammy has but we could surely manage something.'

Ernie's voice exploded in Mandy's ear. 'You can't do a thing like that!' he shouted. 'You can't put a wild creature in a box!'

Mandy and James looked at each other.

'But if you can't manage to do it for us . . .' said Mandy.

Ernie Bell put his head on one side. 'Can't manage?' he said. 'Can't manage? Who said anything about not being able to manage? There isn't a better carpenter in Yorkshire.' He drew himself up and puffed out his chest. 'You give me a couple of days and then bring that little fellow over here. I'll have a run made for him that he won't get out of. But you mark my words, he'll be comfortable in it. Box indeed! I never heard such nonsense.'

Mandy tried to hide her delight. 'Are you sure, Mr Bell?' she said. 'It will be very difficult.'

'Sure?' he said. 'Never mind a couple of days. You bring him over tomorrow morning and you'll see. Now off you go the two of you while I get my tools. I've got work to do!'

'Ernie Bell?' Mr Hope said when they told him. 'You couldn't have found anybody better, but how did you get him to do it? Ernie's the most awkward man I know.'

'Oh, we have our ways,' Mandy said, grinning at James.

They were back at Animal Ark, checking on Lucky. He was still in his cage, looking up at them with the scrap of blue blanket in his mouth. He looked adorable. The blanket was a bit the worse for wear, though. Every day it seemed to get a little smaller. Lucky was very fond of chewing it.

'He's just like a puppy,' said Mandy.

Her dad laughed. 'He's a lot cleverer than a puppy,' he said. 'But that reminds me!'

He went into the cupboard at the end of the room and brought out a dog's lead and collar. 'I don't see why you shouldn't take him for a walk,' he said. 'Just make sure the collar is tight enough. You don't want him escaping in the village!'

Mandy and James slipped the collar round Lucky's neck and clipped on the lead.

'Taking a fox for a walk,' Mandy said. 'That's new.'

'Maybe it'll tire him out,' Mr Hope said. 'He's been out of that cage twice this morning already.'

'Let's take him to see Gran and Grandad,' Mandy said.

Lucky sat there looking up at them, the remains of his blanket still in his mouth.

James laughed. 'He wants to bring his blanket.'

'Of course he can bring it,' Mandy said. 'It's his security blanket.'

Adam Hope smiled. 'I don't know if Welford has seen a stranger sight,' he said as they walked off down the path with Lucky on the lead and the scrap of blue blanket dangling from his pointed little mouth.

'Welford will have to get used to it,' Mandy said.

'At least until Lucky's mother is better.' She looked at her dad. 'She is getting better, isn't she?' she said.

Mr Hope smiled. 'Give her a week or so,' he said. 'Remember it isn't like sending a domestic animal home. She's got to forage for food for herself and for Lucky. There won't be anyone to feed her. And she has to protect herself and her cub from predators.'

Mandy's mouth turned down. *And from traps*, she thought.

'We found the other trap,' she said to her dad.

Mr Hope was all ears. 'Where?' he said.

Mandy and James told him the story. He gave them a lecture about being careful of these things before he told them how terrific they were.

'Who's terrific?' said Emily Hope, coming out of the front door of the house.

'We are,' said Mandy. 'Ask Dad.'

Her mum was getting into her car. 'As if I didn't know that already,' she said. 'I've got a call to make at Sunrise Farm. Do you want a lift anywhere?'

Mandy looked down at Lucky. He was twisting his lead round her ankles.

James bent down to untangle it. 'I'd rather take him for that walk,' he said.

'We're taking him to see Gran and Grandad,' she said. 'I've got to give Gran Mrs Ponsonby's list of stuff she's giving for the auction.'

Mrs Hope laughed. 'It'll be worthwhile going to the auction just to see what Mrs Ponsonby is donating,' she said. 'Bleakfell Hall is the most amazing place I've ever seen. Full of weird and wonderful things.'

'Including Mrs Ponsonby,' James muttered and Mandy giggled.

They waved goodbye and started out for Gran and Grandad's. It took them a lot longer than it should have done to get there. It wasn't just that Lucky wanted to investigate every nook and cranny on the way and sniff at every interesting smell, but people asked how the vixen was getting on. News certainly got around in Welford.

It seemed that the whole village knew Lucky's story.

'Mrs Ponsonby must have told everybody,' said James.

'He's famous,' said Mandy as they came out of the post office. The MacFarlanes who ran it had seen them passing and insisted on them coming in to let them see the little animal.

Even Mr Hardy at the pub had come out to have a

look and insisted on taking a picture of Lucky. 'After all,' he said, 'it is the *Fox* and Goose!'

'Now all you need is a goose,' laughed Mandy.

Mr Hardy patted his camera. 'I'll put this picture up over the bar,' he said. 'If you come across a goose, let me know!'

They got to Lilac Cottage at last.

'So this is Lucky,' Gran said. 'He's so small. What does he eat? We'll have to feed him up.'

'He won't be small for long if he goes on eating at the rate he has been,' said James.

Mandy fished out Mrs Ponsonby's list and handed it to Gran.

'The whole village knows all about him,' she said. 'They think he's wonderful.'

Gran laughed. 'I'm not surprised,' she said. 'Amelia Ponsonby phoned and told me all about that business with the trap and Pandora. She's on the warpath over this trap setting.'

'Good!' said James. 'I hope she catches Mr Western and Dennis Saville.'

Gran laughed again. 'I don't give much for their chances when she sees them again. Now come in and I'll give this list to Tommy to take to the vicar. He's here.'

Mandy and James followed Gran inside. Tommy

Pickard was drinking a glass of milk and eating a slice of sponge cake in the kitchen. Tommy was seven and had just joined the Cub Scouts. He was their keenest member and he wore his uniform as often as he could. He was wearing it now.

'Hi, Tommy,' James said. 'How are your hamsters?'

Tommy answered through a mouthful of sponge cake but his eyes were on Lucky and he was down on his knees at once. 'You've got a new puppy,' he said.

'It isn't a puppy; it's a fox cub!' Mandy said.

Tommy looked up at them, his eyes round, as Lucky nibbled at his fingers and pinched the last of his sponge cake.

'A fox cub?' he said, 'A real fox cub. Wow!'

'He's called Lucky,' said Mandy.

Gran poured glasses of milk and cut wedges of sponge cake for them while she told them all about her new furniture.

'And there are a few other things I can get rid of at the same time,' she said.

'Not get rid of – *donate*, Gran,' Mandy said.

Gran's eyes twinkled. 'Donate,' she said.

Mandy looked round her at Gran's old-fashioned furnishings, her lace table-mats, the jars of dried flowers and shiny, brass ornaments. 'Don't change it too much, Gran,' she said. 'I like it just the way it is.'

Gran laughed. 'Wait till you see my new three-piece suite,' she said. 'It's beautiful.'

But Mandy wasn't so sure she would like it. She was used to Gran and Grandad's cottage looking just the way it did. She even liked their three-piece suite with its big, pink cabbage rose pattern – even if the pattern was a bit faded now and there were a few frayed patches here and there.

It was time to go. Mandy looked round.

'Oh, no,' she said. 'Where's Lucky?'

Tommy looked guilty. 'I just unclipped him for a minute,' he said. All the doors are closed. He couldn't get out.'

They looked everywhere. Under the chairs, behind the sideboard.

'Here he is,' said Tommy, peering into the china cupboard.

Mandy looked in. There was Lucky, peacefully asleep with the blanket between his front paws.

'Oh, look,' she said. 'Isn't he lovely?'

Tommy bit his lip. 'Could we have him as a mascot?' he said.

'What?' said Mandy.

'For the auction,' Tommy said. 'After all he's a

cub and we're Cub Scouts. He could be a good mascot. And he's called Lucky. He might bring us luck. We need luck to raise the money for the new tents. If we can get enough money to buy tents we can go camping this summer just like real scouts.'

Mandy laughed. She didn't point out that Cubs were wolf cubs and that Lucky was a fox cub.

'Why not?' she said.

Tommy beamed. 'Terrific!' he said. 'I'll go and tell everybody!'

'Don't forget the list!' Gran called after him but Tommy was gone.

Gran looked at the list. 'This is destined never to get to where it's going,' she said. 'I'd better take it down myself.' She laughed.

'What are you laughing at?' Mandy said, smiling.

Gran looked at her. 'I was just thinking what an odd auction it's going to be. You should see some of the things Amelia Ponsonby is sending in.' Gran held out the list to Mandy.

'A pedal-organ?' Mandy said as her eyes moved down the list.

'And a fox cub for a mascot. I've never heard anything like it,' said Gran. 'It'll certainly be different!'

Seven

Ernie Bell had been true to his word. The pen he made for Lucky was well-constructed and roomy, and the little cub seemed to take to it immediately.

'See,' Ernie had said proudly when he showed it to them. 'You don't get workmanship like that these days!'

Mandy stood with Lucky in her arms and looked at the pen. It was strong and secure, with the netting stapled firmly to the frame. 'It's perfect, Mr Bell!' she said.

And when they put Lucky in it he scampered around, exploring. Finally he settled down with his blanket.

James laughed. 'Look at him,' he said. 'Mandy's right, Mr Bell. It *is* perfect!'

Ernie Bell scratched his chin and grunted. He was embarrassed at this kind of praise but he was clearly pleased that they liked it so much.

'And we can come and see him every day,' James said.

Ernie looked serious. 'You can come,' he said. 'But I won't have you going feeding him all sorts of rubbish.' The little man drew himself up. 'That there's a wild animal. And you've got to respect that.'

Mandy smiled. They had found the perfect person to look after Lucky.

Mandy and James went every day to Ernie's cottage. After a day or two, word got round the village. Soon Ernie's back garden was full of children coming to see the fox cub. Ernie harrumphed a lot and complained, but Mandy could tell he liked it really.

Tommy Pickard brought a sign to hang on the pen. 'LUCKY', it said, 'WELFORD CUB SCOUTS' MASCOT.'

'You're famous, Lucky!' Mandy said to the little cub on the day before the auction. Ernie had grudgingly allowed Mandy and James to take Lucky to visit Gran and Grandad.

When they got there, Gran was in a whirl of

activity with her spring-cleaning. Mandy and James helped her shift furniture and carry rugs and cushions outside. They got the job of shaking the rugs and beating the cushions.

Lucky, tethered to the gate-post, watched them curiously. He was growing into a fine-looking cub. His coat was reddish-brown now, his eyes alert, and he made little barking sounds when he was excited. But he was still young enough to need a lot of sleep and he curled up in Gran's old china cupboard with his blanket, while Gran gave Mandy and James a well-earned glass of milk each and some of her home-made cakes.

'How is the vixen?' Gran said.

Mandy smiled. 'Much better,' she said. 'Even her coat is looking redder and glossier. She's getting a lot more rest now that she doesn't have Lucky to look after.'

Gran frowned. 'She won't forget about him, will she?'

Mandy shook her head. 'Oh, no. Dad says as soon as she's well enough she'll be as good a mother as any.'

'That cupboard is quite a favourite of Lucky's,' Grandad said as he unhooked yet another pair of curtains for cleaning.

Gran looked at Lucky, snoozing on the bottom shelf of the old wooden cupboard. 'It's being collected for the auction later today,' she said. 'He'll have to find a new place to sleep.'

'We're going down tonight to help sort the stuff out ready for tomorrow,' Mandy said. 'It's amazing. I think everybody in Welford has donated something.'

'Good way to get rid of your rubbish,' Grandad said and winked.

Mandy laughed. 'It's called recycling, Grandad,' she said. 'It's very green.'

'It might be called recycling,' Grandad said, 'but

I'm going to keep a close eye on your gran. There's no telling what she might bring home if the bidding bug bites.'

James looked up and grinned. 'Mrs Ponsonby's pedal-organ?' he said.

Gran laughed. 'I wouldn't have room for it. It would take up the whole of our cottage!'

Mandy looked round her grandparents' cottage. Even topsyturvy as it was at the moment she loved it. It was just right for them.

'You've got enough room for the two of you and a garden and a greenhouse and friends all around,' she said. 'You wouldn't want to live in a place like Bleakfell Hall, would you?'

Gran laughed. 'I certainly wouldn't want to spring-clean it!' she said. 'Now, back to work!'

The village hall was crowded when Mandy and James got there that evening. Mr Hope brought them in the Land-rover, with a load of stuff in the back.

'Are you sure you want to give this to the auction, Mandy?' he said as he lifted down a doll's-house that Mandy had had since she was a little girl.

'It's for a good cause,' said Mandy as she looked at it. She was too old to play with a doll's-house any more, but she would still miss it. Her father had made it for her and she had always loved it. The house stood half a metre high. All the doors and windows opened and the back could be removed to reveal the rooms. When she was younger, Mandy had collected lots of furniture for it. Not just tables and chairs and beds, but tiny plates and cups and even small lifelike figures to make a family.

However, everybody else seemed to be giving something. Her mother had donated a beautiful, old china tea-set and James had two bundles of his favourite comics.

Dad lifted down a box of assorted gardening tools and a bundle of golf clubs that he was donating. 'Right,' he said. 'Let's get this stuff inside.'

James pushed the door of the village hall open and Mandy drew in her breath at the sight.

'It's like Aladdin's cave!' she said. 'Look at all this!'

The village hall was crammed to bursting. There were tables and chairs and toys and books and mirrors. And, in pride of place down at the front of the auctioneer's table, Mandy saw Mrs Ponsonby's pedal-organ, its wood gleaming with years of polishing. There were even a couple of candle-holders on the front of the case.

'And there's Gran's cupboard and her three-piece

suite,' she said, pointing to where the cupboard was wedged in behind a hatstand and a bookcase. Gran had given the suite a good brushing. Mandy looked at the cabbage rose pattern. She would miss that too.

'Who's the auctioneer?' James said.

Mr Hope smiled. 'Walter Pickard,' he said. 'He used to go to cattle auctions when he was a butcher so he knows about these things – or so he says.'

Mandy laughed. 'So long as he doesn't donate a cow or two we'll be all right,' she said. 'I suppose we'd better get started.'

'What do we have to do?' said James.

'First we have to divide things up into lots,' said Adam Hope. He smiled as he saw their faces. 'Bigger items are auctioned on their own. Smaller things are put together.'

'To make lots,' said James. 'Lots of smaller things – that makes sense.'

Mr Hope ran a hand through his hair. 'It isn't quite like that,' he said. 'When you sell something at auction it's called a lot.'

'Even if it's only one thing?' said Mandy.

Mr Hope smiled. 'Confusing, isn't it?' he said.

Mandy grinned. 'Just you tell us what to do and we'll do it,' she said.

Mr Hope nodded. 'Basically you stick a label with a number on each lot and they're auctioned in that order.'

'Oh, is that all?' said James. 'We can do that,' and he grinned at Mandy.

'If it moves give it something to do,' Walter Pickard said, looking at the Cub Scouts bouncing on the springs of an ancient bed. 'If it doesn't move, label it.'

Mandy and James labelled while Mr Walters, the vicar, entered the lots in a ledger. Mr Walters was to keep track of who bought what while Walter conducted the auction.

By the time nine o'clock came Mandy felt she had stuck labels on just about everything in the village hall.

'That's it,' said Mandy as she stuck a label on the very last object. It was an enormous, green, glass vase and it was absolutely hideous. 'Who gave that?' she said.

She looked at James and they spoke together. 'Mrs Ponsonby!' they said.

'Don't forget to bring Lucky tomorrow,' Tommy Pickard said. 'He's going to be our mascot, Grandad.'

Walter smiled at his grandson. 'As if you hadn't told me a dozen times before,' he said.

'Just don't stick a label on him,' Mandy said. 'We don't want to auction him off.'

Tommy grinned.

'Now, now,' said Mr Walters, bustling up. 'Time to go. You youngsters should be getting off home.' He gathered up the Cubs and shooed them out of the door. He paused as he turned to put the lights off in the hall.

'It's looking very nice,' he said.

Mandy took a last look round the village hall. It still looked like Aladdin's cave but now all the treasures were labelled and entered into Mr Walters' ledger. 'It looks great!' she said. 'I'm sure it's going to be a real success!'

The auction started with an opening ceremony. Mrs Ponsonby, Mr Walters and Walter Pickard were seated on the stage. The vicar and Walter looked a bit uncomfortable but Mrs Ponsonby was in her element.

She stood up, looking as pink as her flowery hat, and called the assembled crowd to order.

'Now,' she said, fixing them with her eyes. 'I want you all to dig deep into your pockets and remember what a good cause you are supporting. The Welford Cub Scouts are depending on you. We've all tried very hard to make this event a success.' She drew herself up. 'I myself have donated some things that are very dear to my heart,' and she looked fondly at the pedal-organ. 'And I hope that you have too,' she went on, her voice severe.

Mandy felt very glad she had given the doll's-house. Even so, it hardly seemed enough when Mrs Ponsonby looked at you like that.

'I only gave some comics,' James whispered.

'But it was your collection,' Mandy said. 'You've been saving them for years.'

'And so,' Mrs Ponsonby was saying, 'without more ado . . .'

There was a cough from behind her and the vicar tried to say something. He looked nervous.

Mrs Ponsonby turned majestically towards him. 'What?' she said.

Mr Walters coughed again. 'I think Mr Pickard would like to say a few words,' he said.

Mrs Ponsonby looked down her nose at Walter Pickard. 'Mr Pickard will be talking all afternoon,' she said. 'He is, after all, conducting the auction.' And she turned back to the hall and said. 'I declare the auction open!'

Mandy spluttered with laughter as she saw Walter Pickard's face.

'I hope he didn't want to say anything important,' said James.

'Too bad if he did,' said Mandy. 'With Mrs Ponsonby on her high horse, nobody stands a chance!'

Half an hour later, the auction was going great guns and the lots were falling under the hammer like nine-pins. It really did look as if the day was a runaway success.

Adam Hope was doing afternoon surgery at Animal Ark so he wouldn't be able to get down until late in the afternoon. However, Emily Hope stopped by on her way to Walton and went off loaded with old books and photographs. James's mother and father got an old stone sundial for the garden and Jean Knox bought a big bag of assorted knitting wool. Mandy had a feeling she was going to get a very colourful scarf for Christmas.

Gran and Grandad had dropped in for a while but they couldn't stay too long. The new three-piece suite was being delivered.

'I still like the old one,' Mandy said.

Gran twinkled at her. 'Just you wait till you see the new one,' she said. 'You'll love it!'

Grandad was busy bidding for a stack of flowerpots and a pair of secateurs he thought he could sharpen up.

'Look at that,' said Gran. 'And I'm supposed to be the one that can't resist an auction!'

Mandy laughed. 'What have you bought?' she said.

Gran brought a beautiful little china figure of a fox cub out of her bag. 'For my new china cabinet,' she said. 'It'll remind me of Lucky.' She looked round. 'Where is he?'

Mandy pointed to the little fox cub, tethered to the leg of a nearby chair. He sat there, playing with his blanket. 'He certainly seems to be bringing the Cubs luck,' she said.

'I think everybody is terrified of Mrs Ponsonby,' said Gran. 'Mrs MacFarlane has just bought a set of six microwave cookery books.'

'What's wrong with that?' said Mandy.

'She hasn't got as a microwave!' said Gran and went off chuckling.

'Lucky and Blackie are getting on well,' said James, watching Gran trying to hurry Grandad along.

Mandy looked down. Lucky was curled up under her chair while Blackie sat proudly in the aisle beside him.

'Blackie looks as if he's standing guard over Lucky,' she said.

'He thinks he's a puppy,' said James. Then he

smiled. 'Look what's next!' he said.

Mandy looked. It was her doll's-house. She held her breath as she saw Walter hold it up for everyone to see. She almost blushed with pride as he described it. But she had to admit it was a lovely doll's-house.

The bids came thick and fast. Mandy could hardly believe her ears as the price went up and up.

'Your doll's-house is going to pay for a tent all by itself,' said James.

Mandy listened to the bidding. There were only two would-be buyers left in it now.

She looked round and caught the eye of a little girl. It was Penny Hapwell from Twyford Farm. Penny looked at Mandy. Her eyes were shining with excitement. Her father was sitting beside her – and he was bidding for the doll's-house. Mandy found herself hoping that the doll's-house would go to Penny. She had often played with it when she brought Cally, her kitten, to Animal Ark. She truly loved that doll's-house.

'Who else is bidding?' said Mandy.

James looked around. 'There's a man in the corner,' he said. 'But I don't recognise him.'

Mandy twisted round. A dark-haired man in a suit was bidding for her doll's-house.

'That's a dealer,' said a voice in her ear. It was

Jean Knox. Mandy hadn't realised she was sitting behind them.

'A dealer?' said Mandy.

'He'll buy it and sell it at a fancy price in London, no doubt,' Jean said.

'In a shop?' said Mandy.

Jean nodded. 'More than likely,' she said. 'People collect things like that.'

Mandy's heart sank. 'But I don't want that,' she said. 'I want another little girl to have it – to play with it. I don't want somebody putting it in a collection.'

The bidding stopped. Mandy hadn't been paying attention. She had been too caught up in what Jean had been saying.

'Going . . .' said Walter, 'going . . . gone!'

Mandy held her breath. Who had bought it – the dealer or Penny's dad?

'To Tom Hapwell of Twyford Farm,' Walter said and Mandy felt the smile spreading across her face.

She turned to look at Penny just as the little girl looked across. Penny had a smile as wide as Mandy's own.

James dug her in the ribs.

'Lot thirty-six,' Walter was saying. 'A fine old pedal-organ. Mahogany casing.' He lifted the lid and peered at the organ. 'Two keyboards. And,' he said, hesitating, 'lots of knobs.'

'Knobs!' said a voice. 'They're called stops.' It was Mrs Ponsonby.

'Does it work?' said a voice from the back of the hall.

'Of course it works!' said Mrs Ponsonby.

Mandy turned round. Mrs Ponsonby was talking to Ernie Bell. Mandy wondered if she had been asking him to make a mantrap for Sam Western.

'How do we know?' said the voice again. Mandy twisted round in her seat to see who it was. Mr Hardy, the owner of the Fox and Goose. Mandy grinned. Mr Hardy knew full well who the organ belonged to. He and Mrs Ponsonby didn't get on. Mrs Ponsonby thought a pub was bad for the village.

'Prove it!' Mr Hardy shouted. His eyes were twinkling with mischief.

Mrs Ponsonby rose to her full height and sailed down the hall towards the organ. 'Are you thinking of starting hymn singing at the pub, Mr Hardy?' she said icily.

Mr Hardy grinned good naturedly. 'I was thinking more of music hall tunes, Mrs Ponsonby. If it works, of course.'

Mrs Ponsonby gave him another icy look, lifted a

chair as she passed Mandy and plonked it down in front of the organ.

She pedalled briskly, working up a good head of air, then launched into 'Rock of Ages'. The room resounded to the notes pouring out of the instrument. It didn't only work – it was amazing! Mandy could feel her ears ringing.

Then Mrs Ponsonby started to sing. It was awful. The organ was playing the tune all right. But Mrs Ponsonby seemed to be singing something completely different.

'Ouch!' said James, clamping his hands to his ears.

Blackie set up a howl and a couple of other dogs joined in. With the organ and Mrs Ponsonby and the dogs, the noise was deafening. Only Pandora and Toby seemed to be unaffected by Mrs Ponsonby's singing. Maybe they were used to it, Mandy thought.

There was a scraping of chairs as several people suddenly found they had to leave in a hurry.

'All right, all right. I believe you!' came a shout from the back of the room. But Mrs Ponsonby either didn't hear or refused to take any notice.

Eventually she brought the hymn to a close with a resounding crash of chords and turned triumphantly to Mr Hardy, who had his fingers in his ears.

'Is that proof enough?' she said. 'Or would you like another demonstration – before you buy it?'

Mr Hardy looked resigned. All around him people were trying to hide their amusement. Some weren't bothering to hide it.

'I reckon you got your comeuppance there all right, Bob,' said Ernie Bell, chuckling.

Mr Hardy grinned back. 'I reckon I did, Ernie,' he said. 'So if nobody else is interested I'll give you—'

'There's a minimum price on this lot!' Mrs Ponsonby said majestically. She turned to Walter Pickard, who was enjoying every moment of this. Mandy was almost sure she saw her wink. Mrs Ponsonby? Surely not.

Poor Mr Hardy ended up paying a fortune for the organ.

'It's for a good cause,' Walter said later on. 'He should know better than to tangle with Amelia Ponsonby!'

They were gathering up the unsold items. Just about everybody had left.

Mandy grinned and stretched. She was tired. But the auction had been a great success. There was still a lot of stuff lying around waiting to be collected, but most people had taken their purchases with them.

'Come on, James,' she said. 'Let's get Lucky back to Ernie's.'

She looked down, expecting to see Lucky still curled up with his blanket, tethered to the chair. The lead was still there but it hung slackly. Lucky wasn't under the chair. He wasn't anywhere. Lucky had gone!

Eight

'Where can he have gone?' said Mandy. 'Where is he?'

'He was there all afternoon,' said James, looking at the floor beside Mandy.

Mandy looked round frantically. Nearly everybody had gone. Mrs Ponsonby was still talking to Ernie Bell over by the door. Walter Pickard was starting to clear up and Mr Walters was adding up the figures in his ledger at the auction table. But there was no sign of the little fox cub.

Mr Walters looked up from his ledger. 'We've had a very good day,' he said, beaming at them all. 'I think we'll manage some other camping equipment as well as the tents.'

But Mandy wasn't listening. Her mind was still on Lucky. 'He must be somewhere,' she said. 'Oh, James, if he gets out of the hall he could wander off anywhere! You know how adventurous he is. Anything could happen to him. He could get run over. He could have an accident.' Her eyes opened wide. 'What if there are more of those awful traps around? What if he gets caught in one? We've got to find him!'

'What's all this then?' said Walter Pickard. 'What's the problem?'

Mandy told him swiftly. 'He was here,' she said pointing to the lead still attached to the chair leg beside her.

'We'll look for him,' said Walter. 'Just stay calm and let's do this in an organised way. After all, we can't go losing the Cubs' mascot.'

'Oh,' said Mandy. 'Tommy will be so upset!'

Walter shook his head. 'He will that,' he said. 'He's gone to deliver a couple of things to the MacFarlanes. Let's see if we can find Lucky before he gets back.'

Walter got them organised. They fanned out into a line covering every bit of the hall, looking in boxes and under chairs and even inside the enormous green vase. But there was no sign of Lucky.

'Perhaps he got out of the hall,' Mandy said at last. 'What if we never find him?'

'Now, now,' said Walter, 'don't give up yet, young miss. There are other places to look.'

So they looked under the small stage at the end of the hall and behind the stairwell and in the loos. Mr Hope came back from his afternoon surgery as they were giving up hope of finding Lucky.

'Oh, Dad, he's lost,' Mandy said. 'What if he gets into one of those traps?'

'Hmmph,' said Mrs Ponsonby. 'Just let me get a word with Sam Western and I'll tell him what he can do with those traps!'

Just then the phone rang. Mandy turned hopefully towards the sound. Mr Walters hurried over and picked up the receiver. 'For you,' he said to Adam Hope.

Mandy's father went to take the call while Mandy breathed a sigh. It wasn't news of Lucky then.

'What's the matter?' said a voice from the doorway.

Mandy looked round. It was Tommy. She hesitated. She didn't want to upset him. But he was already looking round the hall.

'Where's Lucky?' he said. 'Where's our mascot? He really was lucky for us, wasn't he, Grandad? Have we made enough money to buy our tents now? Can we go camping this summer?'

Walter looked down at his grandson. 'More than enough,' he said. 'You'll have your summer camp this year.'

'Oh, good!' said Tommy but his eyes were still searching the hall. 'Where's Lucky?' he said again. 'I want to tell him he brought us good luck.'

Walter cleared his throat. 'Lucky has gone and got himself lost,' he said. 'Silly little cub. But he'll turn up, don't you worry.'

Tommy looked puzzled. 'Lost?' he said. Then his face brightened up. 'Oh, I bet he's still in the cupboard. I didn't think he would sleep this long.'

Six faces turned to the little boy – Mandy, James, Mr Hope, Mrs Ponsonby, Walter and Ernie.

'*What?*' they all said at once.

Tommy took a step backwards and looked unsure of himself. 'He was so sleepy,' he said. 'And when Mrs Ponsonby started to play the organ he didn't like the noise. So I unclipped him and put him in the cupboard with his blanket. He likes it in there.'

'Cupboard?' said Walter. 'What cupboard?'

'I think I know,' said Mandy. 'It was Gran's china cupboard, wasn't it, Tommy?'

Tommy nodded. He was beginning to look a little frightened. 'I didn't do anything wrong,' he said. 'It's Lucky's cupboard.'

James smiled down at him. 'That's all right, Tommy,' he said. 'He's probably still there.'

Tommy nodded proudly. 'Oh, he will be,' he said. 'I made sure the door was closed.'

Mandy's breath stopped in her throat and then she remembered that the cupboard had a lattice-work front. At least Lucky would have plenty of air. Then a thought struck her. 'Where is it?' she said to James. 'I didn't see it when we were looking.'

They made a quick tour of all the furniture that was left but the cupboard wasn't there. It had gone.

'But where?' said James.

'What if that dealer bought it?' Mandy said. 'What if he's taken it to London?'

Mr Walters looked up from his ledger. 'We'll soon find out,' he said. 'It's all here in my ledger.'

He took out a pair of half-moon glasses and put them carefully on his nose. Mandy was almost dancing with impatience but she knew there was no point in hurrying him.

James couldn't bear it. He watched Mr Walters' bony finger travel slowly down the length of the list of objects and buyers.

'Let me look,' James said, his own glasses nearly tipping off the end of his nose.

Mr Walters tutted and frowned. 'Now I'll have to start again,' he said. 'You young people have got no patience.'

James looked at Mandy in anguish as the vicar started at the beginning again, finger following the lot numbers down the page, turning each page of the ledger carefully, adjusting his glasses.

At last after what seemed an eternity he said, 'Here it is. Lot number forty-two.'

'Who bought it?' said Mandy.

'Just let me look,' said Mr Walters.

He peered at the page and adjusted his glasses again. 'Ah, the Spry sisters,' he said at last. 'And they took it with them to The Riddings, it says here,' he peered. 'Ernie was doing this bit and I can't read his writing.' Ernie Bell started to say something but Mr Walters went on. 'Oh, yes. Collected by Sam Western,' he said.

'Mr Western?' said Mandy. 'What was he doing here?' Sam Western was much too grand to come to a Cub Scout auction.

'He wanted to talk to the Sprys,' said Ernie. 'He took them home in that posh car of his. I remember now they had some sort of cupboard in the back.'

Mandy and James looked at each other, horrified. One awful thought followed another. It wasn't hard to guess what Mr Western wanted to talk to the Sprys about – the fox-hunting. And poor little Lucky was locked in a cupboard in his car!

'We've got to get him back!' said James.

Mandy nodded. 'And quickly,' she said. She turned to look for her dad.

Adam Hope was striding across the hall in a purposeful way. He stopped as he passed them. 'Look, Mandy,' he said, 'I won't be back for an hour or so. There's a suspected outbreak of staggers at Baildon Farm and I said I'd go up there at once.'

Mandy bit her lip. She had hoped he would be able to take them to The Riddings. 'OK, Dad,' she said.

'I could ring home,' said James as Mr Hope hurried out of the door.

Mandy shook her head. 'We can't waste time waiting,' she said. 'We've got to go there – at once! We've got to get Lucky back!'

'The bikes are outside,' James said. 'How long ago did the Sprys leave?'

Ernie looked doubtful. 'Not more than half an hour,' he said.

'Half an hour?' said Mandy.

James looked at her. 'Time enough for the Sprys to have opened that cupboard,' he said.

'We have to go like the wind,' said Mandy. 'We can't take Blackie. He'll never keep up.'

James turned to Blackie. 'Stay,' he said sternly. Blackie looked up at him and wagged his tail. 'Stay!' said James again even more shortly and the Labrador looked puzzled.

'Come on, James!' said Mandy.

James turned and followed her, leaving Blackie looking sad and lonely. 'Just think of the scare the Sprys will get when they find Lucky,' he said as they made their way out of the hall. 'They'll probably faint with fright.'

'There's an even worse thought,' Mandy said as they got on their bikes and headed off for The Riddings.

'What could be worse?' said James.

Mandy turned a serious face towards him. 'What if Mr Western finds Lucky first?' she said.

Nine

James's straight, brown hair blew back from his forehead as they hurtled past the crossroads at the Fox and Goose and turned on to the Walton Road.

As they passed the pub they could see Mr Hardy standing in front of the pedal organ which was sitting in front of the pub. It looked as if he couldn't get it through the door. He gave them a cheery wave as they passed but Mandy and James had no time to stop. They had to get to The Riddings as fast as possible.

'I wish your dad hadn't had to go out on that call,' said James. 'He could have stood up to Mr Western.'

Mandy's face set. 'He had to go,' she said. 'The staggers can be really serious for cattle. We'll just have to stand up to Mr Western on our own.'

James was breathing heavily as they pedalled up the hill out of Welford.

'What do you think Mr Western will do if he finds Lucky?' he panted.

Mandy gave him a brief look before shooting round the corner at the top of the hill. 'I don't even want to think about it, James!' she called back as she whizzed down the hill.

Pedalling was easier now and in the distance she could see the chimneys of The Riddings rising above the trees. Only a mile to go.

'Oh, please, please, let us be in time,' she muttered to herself. 'Please!'

They left the bikes at the side of the steps and looked up at the massive front door.

'He's still here,' James said pointing to Mr Western's car.

Mandy looked through the car windows. 'No cupboard, though,' she said.

'They must have taken it inside,' said James. 'Unless it's in the boot.'

Mandy bit her lip. 'We'd better look,' she said.

James hesitated. 'It might be locked,' he said.

Mandy thought of poor Lucky locked in a cupboard in the boot of a car. They'd have to take their chances.

'There's only one way to find out,' she said. 'If he's still in there we've got to get him out!'

James pushed his glasses up his nose and took a deep breath. 'OK,' he said. 'You keep a lookout. I'll open the boot.'

Mandy fixed her eyes on the windows at the front of the house. The place seemed deserted, except for Mr Western's car. But The Riddings was so enormous. Mr Western and the Spry sisters could be anywhere.

'It isn't locked,' said James and Mandy turned to him.

'Is he there?' she said eagerly.

James was looking down into the car boot as if turned to stone. Mandy's heart started hammering against her chest.

'What is it, James?' she said. 'What have you found? Is it Lucky? Is he—' She couldn't bear to say it. 'Is he hurt?' she said at last.

James shook his head. 'No,' he said. 'It isn't Lucky. He isn't here and neither is the cupboard.'

'So what *is* there?' said Mandy, puzzled. She

couldn't understand what was making James look like that.

James turned to her. 'See for yourself,' he said.

Mandy came and looked into the boot. For a moment she could hardly speak. 'Traps!' she said. 'More of those horrible traps!'

James turned to her. 'Lucky must be inside,' he said. 'They must have taken the cupboard into the house. I just hope he's still in the cupboard. We've got to get him before Mr Western does!'

Mandy dragged her eyes away from the evil-looking traps. As she did so she thought she caught a movement behind the curtains of the drawing-room window. But she was too worried to pay any attention. 'Right,' she said. 'Let's go!'

'What? We just march up and knock on the door?' said James.

'Why not?' said Mandy. 'Who's going to stop us?'

Just at that moment the front door flew open. 'What are you doing to my car?' said Sam Western, his face red with fury. James shut the boot lid with a crash.

'We want to see Miss Marjorie!'

'Or Miss Joan!' said James.

Mr Western stood at the top of the steps looking down at them. He put his hands on his hips. He looked huge standing up there. 'So you think you'll find them in the boot of my car?' he said.

Mandy opened her mouth to speak but he cut her short. 'I know you two,' he said. 'You're the two young troublemakers from Welford, aren't you? I might have known.'

'We aren't troublemakers,' Mandy began, then she saw a small figure appear behind Mr Western. 'Oh, Miss Joan, we need to talk to you.'

'Make yourselves scarce,' Mr Western said. 'Go on, get out of it before I call the police!' He turned to Miss Joan. 'I've just caught these two in the boot of my car,' he said. 'Up to no good, I'll be bound.'

Mandy bit her lip. 'But we weren't . . .' she began. At that moment Blackie appeared. Patch began to squirm in Miss Joan's arms as Blackie started barking.

'Oh, Blackie!' said James. 'I told you to stay!' He bent down and gave the Labrador a pat. Blackie looked up at him adoringly and wagged his tail.

'And get that animal out of here as well,' Mr Western said. 'Can't you see he's upsetting Miss Spry's cat?' He turned to Miss Joan and ushered her back into the house. 'Young ruffians,' he said to her. 'Don't you worry. They won't get across the doorstep!'

Miss Joan looked worriedly at Blackie. 'Oh, dear,'

she said. 'Patch is so timid. Maybe it would be better if you came back another day, dears. Without your dog.'

'But, Miss Joan!' Mandy began again.

But Mr Western gave them a final look and almost pushed Miss Joan back into the house. 'I want to talk to you about these two,' he said and slammed the door.

James ran a hand through his hair. 'Well,' he said. 'That's that. What on earth are we going to do now?'

Mandy's mouth set. 'We're going to get Lucky out of that cupboard. That's what we're going to do!' she said.

James looked at her. 'You heard Miss Joan,' he said. 'She won't let us in. Not with Blackie here anyway.' He bent down and patted the Labrador. 'Sorry, Blackie. And if we knock on the door again Mr Western will call the police.'

Mandy's eyes sparked fire. 'Maybe that wouldn't be a bad idea,' she said. 'Considering what he's got in the boot of his car. But we don't have time to waste. We've got to get to Lucky as soon as possible. He must still be in the cupboard. The sisters can't know anything about him yet – nor can Sam Western.'

'But they still won't let us in,' said James.

Mandy sighed. 'So, if they won't let us in, we'll have to find another way.'

'What way?' said James.

Mandy frowned, then looked at him very seriously. 'James,' she said. 'I think we're going to have to sneak in.'

James gasped. 'Sneak in?' he said.

Mandy nodded. 'Can you think of any other way of getting in there?'

James shook his head slowly.

'And we *do* have to get into the house,' said Mandy.

James nodded. 'If there's nothing else for it, I suppose we'll have to,' he said.

Mandy looked worried. 'There isn't anything else for it,' she said. 'But first we have to look as if we're doing what we were told to do and go away.' She cast a quick glance over her shoulder and saw a curtain twitch at the drawing-room window, 'Come on,' she said.

'Where?' said James.

'We'll ride down the drive and out of the gates. Then we'll hide the bikes and creep back in through the trees. We can get round to the back of the house without anybody seeing us if we're careful.'

James grinned. 'Mr Western will go mad if he catches us,' he said.

'Then we'll have to make sure he doesn't catch us,' Mandy said. 'Come on. What are you waiting for?'

They hid the bikes among the bushes at the end of the drive and tethered Blackie by his lead to a tree.

'Sorry, Blackie,' James said. 'But we can't have you barking and giving the game away.'

Blackie licked his face happily. He didn't mind. He seemed to think this was a new kind of game.

'You can guard the bikes, Blackie,' said Mandy. 'That's an important job.' She gave the Labrador a pat.

Getting through the trees wasn't all that easy. They grew thickly almost up to the house but provided good cover. They couldn't risk being out in the open. They could see Geoffrey, the gardener, on the far side of the lawn.

'He's weeding,' said James.

'Let's just hope he doesn't turn round as we cross the open space to the house,' Mandy said. She didn't fancy having to explain herself to Geoffrey.

At last they were round the corner of the house. They could see the back door from the shelter of the trees.

'Suppose someone is watching out of a window,' James said.

'We'll have to risk it,' Mandy said. 'Anyway, Mr Western will be in the drawing-room with the Sprys. He thinks we've gone. They won't be looking out of the windows round here.'

'OK,' said James. 'Let's go then!'

They crossed the short open space to the back door quickly but quietly, and sheltered under the portico over the door.

'We've done it!' said Mandy. Then she saw James's face. 'What is it?'

'The back door is locked,' he said miserably.

Mandy sighed. 'How are we going to get in?'

Carefully, trying to make as little noise as possible, they made their way round the house. They tried window after window but all were locked. Mandy was almost in despair when she looked up. There, above her head was a small window – and it was open.

'Look!' she said, pointing.

'We'll never get through that,' said James.

'Oh, yes, we will,' said Mandy determinedly. 'It's our only chance.'

James looked doubtful but Mandy was determined to try.

'I'll go first,' she said. 'Can you give me a leg up?'

'OK,' said James. 'Tell me when you're ready and I'll give you an extra boost.'

James cupped his hands and Mandy put her foot firmly on them and hoisted herself up. Her fingers grasped the window ledge.

'*Now!*' she said, and James shoved with all his strength.

Mandy's fingers gripped hard on the ledge, then she got a foothold in a crack in the wall and she was there, perched on the ledge.

Quickly she thrust one leg over the sill and scrambled through the window. The drop on the other side was bigger than she thought it would be and she landed heavily. 'Ouch,' she said as she hit the floor.

'You all right?' came James's voice from outside.

'Fine,' said Mandy getting up. She could just see the top of James's head over the window ledge. 'Wait, I'll get a chair or something, then I can climb up and haul you up.'

'What room are you in?' James whispered.

Mandy looked round. 'I don't think it's a room at all,' she said. She looked at the jars and bottles and packages on shelves round the walls. 'It looks like a big old-fashioned larder,' she said.

Carefully she opened the door to the room outside – and breathed a sigh of relief. There was nobody there.

She dragged a chair over to the window and scrambled up on it. 'All clear,' she called.

She stretched out her arms and James grasped them round the wrists, climbing with his feet up the wall below the window. With a heave she pulled him through the window and he landed in a heap on top of her when the chair fell over.

'Shh!' said Mandy as James grunted.

'I don't think we'd make very good burglars,' said James.

'Maybe not,' said Mandy, 'but we're the best we've got. Now we've got to look for that cupboard.'

'We'll have to hurry,' said James. 'But quietly.'

On tiptoe they searched downstairs. One by one they opened doors. They found huge, almost empty rooms draped in faded curtains. They tried the last room on the passageway between the dining-room and the hall.

Mandy beckoned to James. 'In here,' she said.

James came and stood beside her. There, in the middle of the huge room was Gran's little china cupboard.

'Listen,' said Mandy. They could hear a very faint

whining sound. 'Lucky!' she said. 'He's there after all!'

She ran to the cupboard, tugging at the door handle until the door opened and Lucky almost fell out in his eagerness at hearing her voice. He began to give sharp little yelps.

'Shh!' said James as Lucky tumbled over himself to get into Mandy's arms. Mandy was hugging him, her face wreathed in smiles.

'Oh, Lucky,' she said. 'It's good to see you!'

Lucky's yelps got louder.

'Hush!' Mandy said to him. 'Somebody will hear you!'

But the little animal was too excited to stop.

Mandy picked up Lucky's blanket. There was a sound in the hall and suddenly the door opened. Mr Western stood there with the Spry sisters behind him.

'What's going on here?' he thundered. Then he saw what Mandy was holding.

Mandy shrank back in fear. Not of Mr Western. She wasn't afraid of him. But beside him were his two bulldogs. They were advancing with teeth bared towards the fox cub in her arms.

Ten

'Drop it!' shouted Sam Western as the dogs advanced on Mandy. 'Drop the cub!'

Mandy looked at him, her mouth set grimly. In front of her the dogs padded across the room from the door, nostrils twitching, scenting the frightened little cub. Then one of them drew back its lips from its teeth and snarled.

'Drop it!' shouted Sam Western again. 'They'll get you as well if you don't!'

The sisters appeared in the doorway.

'Oh, please, do as he says,' Miss Joan said.

Mandy looked at her, standing there with Patch in her arms. The cat was trembling with fright.

Then she looked at the dogs and swallowed hard. 'No!' she said. 'Call them off.'

'I can't call them off!' Sam Western shouted. 'They've got the scent of that fox.' Then he realised Mandy was serious and leaped for his dogs but he was too slow. 'For goodness sake, girl, drop that cub!' he shouted as he tried to reach the dogs.

'No,' said Mandy again.

The dogs were closer now. She saw one of them swing his big head to the side and sniff. Patch quivered in Miss Joan's arms and let out a piteous miaow.

Then the dog gathered himself on his haunches – ready to leap for the poor, defenceless, little cub. Sam Western made a final lunge for the dogs and the two animals sprang.

'Mandy!' James called in terror.

Mandy closed her eyes and held on to Lucky. There was a sudden yowl – and a scream from Miss Joan.

Mandy's eyes flew open in time to see Patch land on the floor. He must have leaped out of Miss Joan's arms. Confused, the little cat ran for cover. But he ran across the path of the dogs. Miss Joan flung herself forward to save her pet. Miss Marjorie grasped her sister's sleeve.

The dogs turned and snarled. They lost interest in the cub and began to chase Patch. But Patch was too quick for them. He gave a heart-stopping screech and raced for the curtains. He scampered up the fraying, dusty material, clinging with his claws. Halfway up, he turned and spat at the dogs.

The dogs bayed and howled at the little cat, jumping at the curtains, tearing them.

Mandy shoved Lucky back into the cupboard.

'Sorry,' she said to the little cub. 'But with these two on the loose this is the safest place for you!'

Mr Western was calling his dogs but they paid no attention. They were leaping at the curtains now.

Dust flew from the ancient material and there was a ripping sound as they gave way.

Patch leaped for safety as the whole lot came down and covered the dogs. Sam Western ran for his dogs just as Patch jumped. The kitten twisted in the air to avoid him but it was impossible. Patch landed on Sam Western's back and sank his claws into his neck. Sam Western let out a roar. His dogs were still entangled in the curtains. They were snarling at each other now. But they couldn't get free of the curtains.

Mandy heaved a sigh of relief.

'Good for you, Patch!' shouted Miss Joan.

Mandy nearly giggled as she watched – except that she was still shaking with fright.

'Are you all right?' said James.

Mandy nodded. 'Let's just get out of here with Lucky,' she said.

Patch sprang lightly from Sam Western's back and padded across the floor to Miss Joan.

'Clever kitty,' said Miss Marjorie as the little cat stalked out of the room.

Sam Western had untangled his dogs now and was clipping their leads on.

'Those two have got a filthy fox cub in that cupboard!' he roared.

'He is not filthy,' said James. 'We gave him a bath the other day.'

'And as for that animal you call a cat!' Sam Western said, rubbing the back of his neck. 'It ought to be put down.'

'How dare you say that about Patch, Mr Western?' Miss Joan said.

'Mr Western,' said Miss Marjorie, outraged. 'Control yourself!'

Mandy looked round the room. The dogs were growling. Mr Western was mopping the blood on his neck with his handkerchief. The sisters were looking very angry indeed. And James had come to stand beside her and the cupboard.

'Ask what they've got in that cupboard,' said Mr Western. 'Go on ask. Filthy vermin.'

'Mr Western!' said Miss Marjorie.

Mr Western looked furious. 'I mean the fox cub,' he said. 'If you let me use your land for hunting you won't have all this nonsense.'

'You can't!' said Mandy to the Spry sisters. 'You can't let him do it! He's already setting traps for them. Do you remember when we brought the vixen and fox cub here? It was Mr Western that set that trap!'

'And we found another one the other day,' said

James. 'We got to it just in time to stop Mrs Ponsonby's peke getting hurt.'

'So it was you who sprang those traps!' said Mr Western, his face black as thunder. 'Just wait till . . .' and he took a few threatening strides towards them.

Miss Marjorie's voice was hard as she said. 'You set traps, Mr Western?'

Sam Western stopped in his tracks. Mandy could see him realise what he had said. 'No, no,' he said. 'My manager may have done – without my knowing – but I know how much you disapprove of traps. Hunting is a very different matter.'

'I'm very glad to hear it,' Miss Joan said.

'Dear Papa always said hunting was for gentlemen but traps were not,' said Miss Marjorie.

'He did set them, or at least he knew about them,' said James.

Sam Western turned to him. 'I'd advise you to keep quiet, young man,' he said. 'Anyone who has broken into a house should say as little as possible.'

Mandy stepped forward. 'It's easy enough to prove,' she said. 'All we have to do is look in the boot of his car. There are more traps there.'

'Nonsense!' said Mr Western, clearly rattled. 'Pack of lies.'

Mandy took a step forward. 'Why don't we let Miss

Joan and Miss Marjorie see for themselves?' she said.

'Outrageous,' said Mr Western. 'The cheek of it. I don't have to agree to anything.'

'Perhaps not,' said Miss Joan quietly, 'but it would make us wonder why you are so reluctant to show us what is in the boot of your car.'

Mr Western spluttered but he knew he was beaten. 'I don't know why you're so bothered about them,' he said. 'You set traps to catch vermin and foxes are just vermin.'

'It's because the traps are so cruel, Mr Western,' said Miss Marjorie quietly. 'And I think you are a cruel man. To set those dogs on a child!'

'I didn't,' said Sam Western. 'I told her to drop the cub.'

'As if I would!' said Mandy.

Miss Joan turned to her. 'I think Mandy has shown us what caring for animals is really about,' she said.

'She was ready to defend that little cub to the last,' said Miss Marjorie.

'If she is willing to do something like that,' said Miss Joan, 'how can we allow you to kill foxes on our land?'

'You know, I begin to think that perhaps Father was wrong,' said Miss Marjorie.

Miss Joan looked a little shocked but she supported

her sister. 'No matter what we think about fox-hunting,' she said, 'we certainly could not allow you on to our land – not after this, Mr Western. We are all God's creatures, you see, and we really have no right to kill these animals.'

'We can see that now – thanks to Mandy,' said Miss Marjorie.

'So if you would be so good as to go away now,' said Miss Joan.

'And please don't come back,' said Miss Marjorie.

A face suddenly appeared at the window. Geoffrey, the gardener. He looked at the curtains lying inside the room and pushed his cap back on his head.

'Been a bit of a to-do, then?' he said, scratching his head.

'You could say that, Geoffrey,' said Miss Joan.

Geoffrey looked at Sam Western and his dogs. 'Need any help then?' he said.

'Mr Western was just leaving,' said Miss Marjorie with all her dignity.

The gardener put his cap back on his head. 'Good,' he said. 'Never did like him – or his dogs,' and he stomped off across the lawn.

Mandy saw Mr Western open his mouth to try to speak but he was lost for words.

'Heel!' he said to his dogs and Mandy watched

him stride out of the room into the hall and down the steps to his car. She suddenly remembered something and rushed after him.

'If we find any more of these traps,' she shouted, 'we shall know where to send the police.'

Mr Western turned to her. 'Namby-pamby animal lover,' he said. 'Just you stay out of my way in future! I always knew you were a troublemaker!'

Mandy came back into the room to find the sisters cooing over Lucky whom James had released from the cupboard.

'He's as good as new,' said James. 'Being in the cupboard hasn't done him a bit of harm.'

Mandy smiled. 'He always did like that cupboard,' she said.

'Oh, look at him!' said Miss Marjorie. 'His coat is quite red now.'

'And he still has the blanket we gave him,' said Miss Joan. 'How sweet.'

The twins looked at each other over the cub's furry head. 'How could anybody want to hunt down a sweet little creature like this?' said Miss Joan.

Miss Marjorie shook her head. 'It's positively wicked,' she said. 'Now, who would like a cup of tea?'

Mandy looked at James and smiled. He looked as relieved as she felt. They could relax now. There would be no more traps for animals and no fox hunting in Welford. She looked down at the cub in her arms.

'You *are* Lucky,' she said. 'Lucky for yourself and lucky for all the other little fox cubs you're going to save from being hunted.'

Lucky gave a short bark, his eyes as bright as buttons.

Mandy laughed. 'Come on!' she said to the little creature. 'We'll see if we can get you some bread and milk.'

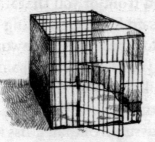

Eleven

After Mr Western had gone Miss Joan turned to Mandy and said, 'We would like it very much if Lucky and his mother could be released on to our land – when the time comes.'

'Yes, indeed,' Miss Marjorie said. 'We feel responsible for them somehow.'

'If it hadn't been for us not standing up to Mr Western none of this would have happened,' said Miss Joan.

'Oh, no,' Mandy said. 'You mustn't think that. You couldn't have stopped him laying those traps.'

'In fact,' James put in, 'if all this hadn't happened we wouldn't have proof that he was the one laying the traps. It was just our word against his. But now he's admitted in front of you that it was him.'

'So you see,' said Mandy, cuddling Lucky, 'it really all worked out for the best. There won't be any more traps now and your land will be safe for foxes.'

'Indeed it will,' said Miss Joan with spirit. 'There will be no hunting on our land.'

'You can rest assured of that!' Miss Marjorie added.

'And I can't think of anywhere I'd rather let them go than here at The Riddings,' said Mandy. 'If it hadn't been for you letting Mum work in your kitchen, Lucky's mother might not have survived at all – and then Lucky wouldn't have survived either.'

The sisters looked pleased.

Then Mandy and James took Lucky back to Ernie Bell's house. Ernie chuckled when they told him how the sisters had stood up to Mr Western.

'And you mark my words,' he said as he put Lucky gently back in his pen, 'Sam Western won't dare to lay any more traps now. There are too many of us as know about it for him to go around doing a thing like that again.'

Ernie looked at the little cub scampering about his pen, none the worse for his adventure. 'I'll miss him when he goes,' he said. 'But he's a wild creature and the wild is the place for him.'

'We're going to release him and his mother on the Sprys' land,' said Mandy.

Ernie smiled. 'They'll find good cover there,' he said. 'You let me know when and I'll come with you.'

'Great!' said James. 'We can give them a real send-off!'

Mandy turned to him, her face alight. 'Who else will we invite?' she said.

James grinned. 'Everybody who's been interested in Lucky,' he said.

Mandy shook her head. 'That's nearly the whole village,' she said. 'The Spry sisters are shy, remember.'

James looked thoughtful. 'Not as shy as they used to be,' he said. 'Remember when they first adopted Patch?'

Mandy nodded. Adopting the kitten had made a real difference to the sisters.

'If we gather all the people together who really cared for Lucky and his mother,' James said, 'they won't be shy of them – how could they be?'

Mandy's face brightened. 'I think you're right,' she said. 'Who shall we start with?'

'Your gran and grandad?' said James.

'Let's go and tell them,' said Mandy.

* * *

Lilac Cottage was as neat as a new pin when they arrived. All the havoc of spring-cleaning had gone, leaving the cottage in shining apple pie order. Mandy and James gave Gran their news as they tumbled into the cottage with Blackie at their heels.

'You can count on us to be there,' said Gran. 'Now, what do you think of my new three-piece suite?'

Mandy looked round and gasped at what she saw.

'Gran?' she said, staring at the new three-piece suite.

'I told you you would like it,' said Gran.

'But it's the same as the old one,' Mandy said.

'As near as makes no difference,' said Gran. 'I always liked the old one.'

Mandy looked at the familiar cottage, at the new suite with its pattern of cabbage roses.

'Of course it isn't frayed like the old one – or faded,' said Gran.

Mandy laughed. 'Nothing's changed, Gran,' she said. 'It's all just the same.' And she felt a warm glow. She hadn't wanted Lilac Cottage to change – not the tiniest bit.

'Some things change,' said Gran. 'Your dad says Lucky's mother is coming on a treat now. It won't be long before she's ready to leave Animal Ark.'

Mandy felt a swift pang of sadness. Then she

remembered what Ernie Bell had said. He was right – wild creatures belonged in the wild.

And soon it was time to say goodbye to Lucky and his mother. Mr and Mrs Hope had both come to The Riddings. The Sprys had laid on tea and delicious home-made cakes.

The sisters were dressed in their Sunday best. Miss Joan had a large, floppy, straw hat with a bunch of flowers weighing down the brim. Miss Marjorie looked wonderful in a long silk skirt and frilly blouse. Even Geoffrey had turned out for the occasion. He was dressed in his best tweed jacket and a brand-new pair of Wellington boots.

Gran and Grandad were there too, and Ernie Bell and Walter Pickard and Tommy.

They were all gathered outside The Riddings. The Spry sisters were in a flutter of nervousness when Mrs Ponsonby arrived. She got out of her car with Toby and Pandora at her heels. Blackie immediately went over to play with them.

'Oh, no,' James muttered to Mandy. 'I hope he behaves!'

'Call him,' said Mandy.

James looked at her. 'And show Mrs Ponsonby how disobedient he is?' he said. 'She would have

Blackie signed up for those obedience classes in no time!'

Mrs Ponsonby came towards them like a ship in full sail. 'I just came to tell you, Miss Joan and Miss Marjorie,' she said, 'that I have spoken most severely to Mr Western. I explained that he is not under any circumstances to bother you again with this nonsense about fox-hunting!'

The Spry sisters fluttered even more. 'That was very kind of you, Mrs Ponsonby,' said Miss Joan.

Mrs Ponsonby drew herself up. 'Not at all,' she said. 'The man had to be taught a lesson. And let me tell you that the whole of Welford admires you for standing up to him.'

Miss Joan and Miss Marjorie went quite pink at the compliment. Then Ernie Bell broke in.

'Maybe you should get Sam Western along to those obedience classes of yours at the village hall,' he said and chuckled.

Mrs Ponsonby looked down her nose at him. 'I have decided,' she said, 'that I will not be running the obedience classes after all.'

Mandy heard James gasp.

'Why would that be, Mrs Ponsonby?' Mr Hope said, with a twinkle in his eye, 'I thought you were a great believer in training animals.'

Emily Hope nudged her husband. 'Don't tease,' she said.

But Mrs Ponsonby was speaking again. 'If you must know, it was these two who changed my mind,' she said, looking at Mandy and James.

'Us?' said Mandy, feeling puzzled.

'Certainly,' said Mrs Ponsonby. 'If Toby had come when he was called then Pandora would have gone to investigate that trap. It was Toby being disobedient that saved my precious Pandora.' She looked at where Toby and Pandora were rolling in a patch of mud with Blackie.

Mandy saw her open her mouth to call the dogs, then close it again. 'Obedience isn't everything,' Mrs Ponsonby said firmly.

'No obedience classes?' said James. He sounded as if he could hardly believe it.

Mrs Ponsonby gave him a look. Then she turned towards Blackie, who was digging a hole in a flower-bed and encouraging Toby and Pandora to do the same.

Geoffrey saw them too. 'Get out of there!' he shouted.

'Of course I could make an exception for Blackie,' Mrs Ponsonby said.

'Oh, no!' said James. 'Don't. I mean, don't bother,

don't trouble yourself.' He sprinted over to get hold of Blackie and drag him back.

Mrs Ponsonby turned to Mandy and this time there was no mistake. She definitely *did* wink. Mandy giggled.

'Time to let these two go,' said Adam Hope as he lifted two cages out of the back of the Land-rover.

Mandy's giggles stopped abruptly. Now she would have to say goodbye to Lucky and his mother.

'I think you two should do it,' said Mrs Hope to Mandy and James.

Ernie Bell took hold of Blackie's collar and Adam Hope gave the cage with the vixen in it to James. Then he bent and picked up the cage with Lucky in it. 'This is your job, Mandy,' he said.

Mandy looked at the little fox cub. He had grown so much in the last weeks. His coat was russet, his ears pricked and alert and his eyes were bright and intelligent as he looked at her. She swallowed. She couldn't speak.

'Let them go in amongst the trees,' said Ernie Bell. 'They'll be more at home there. And it'll be quieter. Not so many people around.'

Mandy looked at him gratefully. He understood that she wanted to be by herself when she let Lucky go.

'You go ahead,' said Gran. 'I want to talk to Miss Marjorie and Miss Joan about these delicious cakes.'

'If you want the recipe, we'd be only too glad,' said Miss Marjorie.

Gran looked at the sisters. 'Oh, I couldn't make them as well as you do,' she said. 'No, I was wondering if you would help out at my baked goods stall at the church bazaar next month – and bake some cakes for it, of course.'

'Us?' said Miss Joan. 'Oh, we've never done anything like that before.'

Grandad smiled. 'There's nothing to it,' he said. 'And, besides, you'd be among friends.'

'There's always someone to help if you need it,' said Emily Hope. 'I'm doing the tombola.'

'And I'm in charge of the bottle-stall,' said Ernie Bell.

'And I'm down for the bookstall,' said Adam Hope.

Gran said gently, 'You really would be among friends.'

Miss Marjorie and Miss Joan looked at each other.

'I suppose we could,' said Miss Marjorie.

'It would be quite fun,' said Miss Joan, looking surprised at herself.

Mandy looked round the circle of faces, all intent

on the Spry sisters. She didn't think it would be long before the sisters were part of village life. Not if Gran had her way.

Now was the moment. She and James could slip away quietly while the church bazaar was being discussed.

Carefully they carried the cages to the edge of the trees and carefully they set them down on the grass.

'I suppose we have to let them go,' said James. He was looking sad too.

Mandy nodded. 'Now?' she said. It was better to get it over with. She didn't think she could bear to drag it out.

'Now,' said James and together they lifted the latches on the cages.

For a moment nothing happened. Then the vixen sniffed the air delicately and stepped neatly out of her cage. Her coat gleamed in the sun and her ears stood straight and pricked for every sound. She turned this way and that, her eyes bright with health. She moved forward gracefully. She showed no sign of her injury now – not even the slightest limp.

Then Lucky pattered out of his cage and ran to her. Gently she nudged him and he nuzzled her flank. Then she bent her head and gave him a push

and made a low sound deep in her throat. He looked up at her and gave a sharp little bark in answer. Then all at once they were off, fast as the wind, heads up, tails flashing, running side by side through the trees, free as the air.

Mandy watched until they were no more than a blur through her tears. Then, at the edge of the densest part of the trees, the vixen stopped and turned. Lucky also stopped and looked back. Clear on the air came a high-pitched bark. Again and again it came.

Mandy felt the tears roll down her cheeks. She would miss Lucky so much. But she knew that a wild animal belonged in the wild. She wouldn't want Lucky caged, petted. She wanted him to be free – free as the wind that rustled the branches over her head. Free to roam and to wander and to live out his life the way nature intended him to. But it hurt to let him go.

Still the barking went on – until Mandy raised her hand and answered.

'Goodbye, Lucky,' she said as the two animals turned and were lost in the depths of the wood. 'Goodbye. Stay safe!'

LUCY DANIELS
Owl
—*in the*—
Office

Illustrations by Shelagh McNicholas

*Hodder
Children's
Books*

a division of Hodder Headline plc

Owl in the Office

Special thanks to Tom Tyrell of the Tomar Owl Sanctuary

Text Copyright © Ben M. Baglio 1995
Illustrations Copyright © Shelagh McNicholas 1995
Created by Ben M. Baglio, London W6 0HE

First published as a single volume in Great Britain in 1995
by Hodder Children's Books

To Rats and Jess and their cousins,
Midge and Milo

One

'Quick, James – over here!' Mandy Hope shouted to her friend, James Hunter. She knelt down in a pile of last autumn's fallen leaves, gently brushing some aside.

Mandy and James were out walking in Monkton Spinney near Welford, the Yorkshire village where they lived. Mandy had spotted something in the carpet of leaves beneath one of the oak trees.

'What have you found?' James ran over and skidded to a halt beside her. His trainers sent up a spray of leaves. He pushed his glasses back up his nose and looked down at the little hollow Mandy had made in the leaves.

Mandy cupped her hands together and lifted something very carefully from the ground. She held what looked like a bundle of bedraggled feathers. Two round, dark eyes stared at James. A sharp, hooked beak opened and a kind of creaky noise came out. It sounded like a gate that needed oiling. Mandy drew in her breath. She gazed up at James with shining eyes.

'Oh! Look, it's a baby owl.'

James touched the tiny creature gently with his fingertip. 'What kind of owl is it?'

'A tawny owl, I think,' said Mandy. 'Oh, the poor thing!' She had thought it might be an owl when she first spied the bundle of grey-brown flecked feathers lying in its hollow of leaves. Although she'd seen pictures of baby owls she had never actually seen a live one. It felt soft and beautiful and very fragile.

'Wow!' exclaimed James. His eyes were round behind his spectacles. 'Where did it come from, Mandy?'

Mandy looked up into the huge oak tree, its great branches reaching up to the sky.

'Up there somewhere,' she said, frowning. 'You can never really see owl's nests; they're too well hidden. It's probably where two of those big branches meet or maybe in an old squirrel's drey somewhere.'

Mandy's heart jolted with pity. 'Poor thing,' she murmured again.

James squinted upwards, pushing back the peak of his baseball cap to get a better view. 'Maybe we could climb up and put it back in its nest,' he suggested hopefully.

Mandy knew it would be the best solution. The owl wouldn't survive for long out in the open, that was for sure. But how on earth were they to reach it?

'We'd need a ladder.' Mandy tucked a strand of blonde hair behind her ear. Her brows knitted together over her blue eyes in a thoughtful frown. 'Or maybe I could climb up?' she said, not sounding at all sure. She had long legs and was pretty good at climbing trees but this one had a tall, straight trunk with no footholds at all.

'No way,' said James with a shake of his head. 'The first branch is miles up. Don't you think we should just leave it where it is?'

Mandy stared at him in horror. 'We can't do that! It'll get eaten by a fox or something!'

James shrugged. 'I read somewhere you should

leave baby birds alone. Sometimes their parents come down to feed them.'

Mandy shook her head. 'Owls mostly come out at night,' she said. 'It could be too late by the time they find him.' She heaved a sigh. There was only one thing to do then. They would have to take the baby owl back to Animal Ark. Her mum and dad were both veterinary surgeons. They would know what to do.

'We'll have to take it back with us.' she said to James.

James bit his lip. Once Mandy made up her mind about something, there was no changing it.

James whistled to his dog. Blackie crashed through the undergrowth towards them.

'Come on, Blackie.' James patted the Labrador's sleek head. 'Time to go home.'

But Blackie was too interested in Mandy's mysterious bundle to take any notice of his master. He jumped up, sniffing the owl's feathers.

'Down,' Mandy commanded. Blackie ignored her and went on sniffing.

James pulled his collar gently. 'Blackie, do as you're told!'

Blackie wasn't the most obedient dog, but this time he listened to James and allowed himself to be pulled away from the baby owl.

Mandy carefully wrapped the owlet in her scarf and cradled it gently in her arms. 'Come on then, James. The sooner we get this little thing into the warm, the better.'

Blackie soon lost interest and trotted on ahead.

'What do you feed owls on?' James trudged along by Mandy's side as they made their way through the spinney, out towards the road that led to the village of Welford.

Mr and Mrs Hope ran a busy veterinary practice in the village. They had adopted Mandy when she was a baby. Her natural parents had been killed in a car crash and Mandy couldn't remember anything about them. The Hopes were the only parents Mandy had ever known. As far as she was concerned nobody could wish for a better mother or father.

James, a year younger, was Mandy's best friend. He shared her love of animals. Mandy and James both went to school in the neighbouring town of Walton. Today though, was the first day of the spring half-term.

'I'm not sure,' Mandy said in answer to James's question. She knew that in the wild, owls hunted for small mammals like mice and voles. Owls hunted mostly at night, although sometimes you saw them out in the daytime, especially during springtime when they had young to feed. But Mandy couldn't exactly imagine catching little furry animals to feed the baby owl. In fact Mandy wasn't sure *what* she was going to do with it. All she knew was that they couldn't leave the tiny, helpless creature out in the woods with no one to protect it.

The bird peeped out with huge, scared eyes as they made their way across the village green towards the old stone cottage with its wooden sign that said 'Animal Ark, Veterinary Surgeon'. Mr and Mrs Hope had started the practice when they got married. Mr Hope had lived in Welford all his life and both he and his wife were well known and popular members of the village community.

Mandy and James hurried in through the surgery door. Jean Knox, the receptionist, was busy at her computer. She looked up as Mandy and James burst in.

'Where's Mum and Dad?' Mandy asked breathlessly, cradling the owlet against her coat.

Jean glanced at the diary in front of her. 'Your dad's gone up to Syke Farm and your mum's indoors.' She peered over the top of her glasses.

'What *have* you got there, Mandy?'

Mandy went closer and gently peeled back the woolly scarf.

Jean's hand flew to her mouth. 'Oh, my goodness. Where did you get that?'

Mandy explained quickly.

'We couldn't possibly reach the owl's nest,' James blurted. 'So we had to bring it here.'

'Well, whatever next. Take it out to Simon. He'll know what to do for the best,' Jean said matter-of-factly. It was no real surprise to her when Mandy arrived home with a sick or abandoned animal. If Mandy had arrived home with a baby elephant, Jean probably wouldn't have batted an eyelid. Mandy loved all animals and wanted to be a vet herself one day.

Simon, the veterinary nurse, was sterilising the surgical instruments. It had been a busy morning: a cat with a thorn in its paw; a dog that had swallowed a sock; five puppies for injections; a rabbit with pneumonia and a gerbil whose babies were ready to be born. Then to cap it all, fussy Mrs Ponsonby from Bleakfell Hall had arrived with Pandora, her pampered Pekinese, just as they were closing. It had taken all of Mrs Hope's powers of persuasion to convince Mrs Ponsonby that her dog didn't have flu, just a runny nose.

Simon looked up and grinned when Mandy and James walked in.

'Hello, you two,' he said cheerily. 'What have you been up to this morning?'

'We found this . . .' Mandy pulled back the scarf to reveal the baby owl.

'Oh, wow!' Simon touched the creature's head. 'Where?'

James explained.

Simon frowned and ran his hand over his fair hair. 'You know, you should really have left him there.'

'I *told* you!' James said.

Mandy began to wonder if she had done the right thing in bringing the owl to the surgery. But it was too late now. Rightly or wrongly she had brought him home and it was now her responsibility to look after him. 'But I couldn't just leave him,' she protested.

Simon pulled a wry face. 'I know it's hard, Mandy, but the parents may have come down to feed him – or he might have been able to find his way back to the nest.'

Mandy shook her head firmly. 'No, I'm sure he's too weak for that.'

Simon looked at the tiny creature. 'Well, maybe

you're right. If he's the smallest chick the others probably hogged all the food and he probably would have starved to death anyway.'

Simon pulled back the scarf a little more. 'He's very tiny. I'm afraid it's the survival of the fittest where birds in the nest are concerned. Nature can be very cruel at times.'

'It certainly can,' Mandy said. The little owl looked so sweet. To never have known if it lived or died would have been too much to bear.

'I think the best thing to do . . .' Simon suggested, 'is to take the little fellow up to the animal sanctuary. I'm sure Betty Hilder will know what's best.'

Just then, Emily Hope came through the door. She was still wearing her white vet's coat, and her red hair was tied up with a green silk scarf. She smiled. 'Hi, you two.' Then she spied the small bundle in the crook of Mandy's arm. 'What have you brought us now, Mandy?'

Mandy quickly explained.

'Simon says we should have left him there,' said James.

Mrs Hope raised her eyebrows. 'Yes, you should have done really. But now he *is* here, let's take a look at him.'

'Simon suggested we take him up to Betty,' said Mandy.

Mrs Hope agreed. 'Good idea,' she said. 'I'll take a look at him first though. He could be injured. Was he just lying on the ground?'

'Well, he was *sitting* on the ground,' Mandy said. 'In fact,' she added, 'I almost trod on him.'

'OK,' Mrs Hope said in her usual businesslike manner. She took a pair of surgical gloves out of their sealed polythene packet and pulled them on. 'Sit up on the couch, Mandy and I'll take a look at him.'

Mandy heaved herself up. She gently unwrapped the little owl and set him carefully on her knee. Free of the woolly scarf, he shook his feathers, staggered and almost fell. His sharp claws gripped the knee of Mandy's jeans as he struggled to regain his balance.

Mandy put her hands either side to steady him, smoothing down the soft feathers. She was surprised to feel how tiny his body was. The owl sat there blinking in the bright overhead light. Then, without warning, he flapped his wings and tried to fly, overbalancing completely and landing in a heap on the scrubbed tiles of the surgery floor.

Mandy jumped down and bent to retrieve him,

worried in case the owl had landed awkwardly. It would be too bad if the little bird had survived its fall from the nest then ended up hurting itself on the surgery floor!

'Mind those talons,' her mother warned. 'You might get a nasty scratch.'

Mandy put her hands either side of the bird's wings. 'Now, behave yourself, Mr Owl,' she said sternly. The owl blinked at her and made a squeak. Mandy couldn't help smiling. He looked rather indignant at being handled by a human being! She set him down on her knee again. This time, he stayed where he was.

Mrs Hope quickly examined the bird. Feet, wings, fluffy head. Finally she smoothed down its feathers. 'He's very thin,' she said, frowning. 'Skin and bone. I reckon he hasn't been getting much food. Just wrap him up again, Mandy. I'll take a look at his eyes and beak.'

'Mum, can't I keep him here?' Mandy said. 'I'll look after him, I promise. I'll get food for him and everything.'

Mrs Hope shook her head. 'Sorry, Mandy. Looking after baby owls is really very specialised. Simon's right, we'd better take it to the sanctuary. Betty will know what's best.'

Mandy knew better than to argue with her mother. A veterinary surgery was no place to keep a baby owl. However much Mandy longed to take care of it, she knew expert help was needed.

Mrs Hope looked at her watch. 'I could take you up there now if you like. I haven't got any calls to make until a bit later.'

'That would be great, Mum. Thanks.' Mandy got down off the couch. 'Coming, James?'

'You bet!'

'You'd better put Blackie in the back,' Mrs Hope told James when they got outside. Blackie was still trying to find out what Mandy had in her arms, jumping up and sniffing at the scarf. 'He seems a bit too nosy if you ask me.'

Blackie was always curious about everything. And his curiosity often got him into trouble.

James opened the rear door of the four-wheel drive and banged his hand on the floor. Blackie jumped inside.

'Stay!' James commanded.

For once, Blackie did as he was told. He sat looking out of the window, his tail wagging like mad. Every trip in a car was an adventure to him.

They all piled in and Mrs Hope set off through the village. She turned off past the post office, heading for the narrow hill road that led up to the Welford Animal Sanctuary.

'Mum,' Mandy said when they were halfway there. She had been feeling a bit upset about taking the owl away from its natural environment. 'I'm sorry if I've done the wrong thing.'

Mrs Hope patted her knee. 'It just might be better to ask someone's advice next time, that's all.'

'I will,' Mandy promised. She made a vow to listen to James a bit more too. She couldn't *always* be right.

Mandy had been to the sanctuary several times

before and knew its owner, Betty Hilder, very well. Although she loved seeing the animals Betty had rescued, her heart always went out to them. She knew that most of them would have had to be put to sleep if Betty hadn't taken them in. There were creatures of every kind. Dogs, cats, donkeys, a Shetland pony, an ancient goat with three legs. The last time Mandy had been there, Betty even had a Vietnamese pot-bellied pig that someone had brought in.

'They had bought it as a pet,' Betty had explained to Mandy. 'No one ever told them that pigs are extremely difficult to house-train.'

The car crested the summit of the hill and began the winding descent down the other side.

Mandy gazed out of the car window at the panorama of hills and dales. The dry-stone walls made a picturesque pattern across the landscape. The sky was blue and broad, not a cloud to be seen.

Mandy loved it up here on the moor, the village of Welford spread out below. There were the two roads, the church and the village green in the middle. A pall of smoke rose from the row of quaint old cottages behind the Fox and Goose pub. Her grandad's friend, Walter Pickard, lived in one.

They'd both been bell-ringers at the church for years. Mr Pickard must be having a bonfire, burning his garden rubbish probably. The village people took great pride in their gardens and Walter grew roses that won prizes at the Welford Show every year.

Mrs Hope changed gear and swung the four-wheel drive round into the drive that led up to the sanctuary. To Mandy's dismay, the gate was shut and locked.

'Oh!' she exclaimed, puzzled. 'I've never seen it shut before.'

Mandy wondered what on earth had happened. Betty was always proud to be able to say the sanctuary was open any time.

Mrs Hope pulled up in front of the gate. 'Maybe she's gone out shopping,' she suggested. 'I'll just get out and see.'

Mrs Hope went up to the gate. She stood frowning at the rows of kennels and outbuildings that housed the rescued animals. Then, Betty Hilder, a young woman dressed in baggy jeans and a thick jumper, came out of her bungalow and hurried to open the gate. She spoke to Mrs Hope.

'I wonder what they're talking about,' said James.

'I don't know,' said Mandy, still worried. 'Betty looks a bit upset.'

Betty took out a key and unlocked the gate. Mrs Hope came back to the car looking grim. As soon as she opened the door they bombarded her with questions.

'What's up, Mum?' asked Mandy, her heart pounding. She had a feeling something really serious was going on.

'Why is Betty looking so upset?' asked James.

Mrs Hope turned on the ignition. 'I'm afraid it's bad news, you two,' she said. 'Betty's letting *us* in but she's had to close the sanctuary to the general public.'

Mandy leaned forward anxiously. 'Closed! Mum . . . why?'

Mrs Hope drove through the gate and into the concrete yard. A chorus of dogs greeted the newcomers as they got out of the car. In the back, Blackie barked excitedly and clawed at the window.

'Quiet, Blackie!' James commanded.

'Betty's very short of money,' Mrs Hope told Mandy and James as she shut the car door. 'She just can't afford to keep things going.'

'What will happen to the animals?' said Mandy. She glanced down at the tiny, helpless bundle in her arms. If Betty wasn't going to be able to look after the baby owl then who would? There wasn't another sanctuary for miles.

Her mother glanced at her. 'If they can't be found homes, then—' She broke off. Mandy had a horrible sinking feeling she knew exactly what her mum was going to say. If the animals couldn't be found homes then they would all have to be destroyed!

'No!' Mandy turned to James. 'We can't let the animals be put to sleep,' she cried. 'We've got to do something. We've just *got* to!'

Two

As Mandy went towards the bungalow clutching her precious bundle, Betty pulled back the scarf and took a peek at the owl.

'Poor thing,' she said. 'Bring it into the office, Mandy. It's warmer in there.'

They went into the room where Betty kept her old typewriter and telephone. There were papers all over the desk, photos of cats and dogs on the wall and a bucket of pony nuts in one corner.

Two cats came over and rubbed themselves against Mandy's legs. Betty shooed them out. She went through another door and brought back a large cage with a wooden back. 'We'll put him in this hospital cage for the time being,' she said. 'He's got to be isolated in case he's carrying any pests or diseases.'

Mandy handed over her precious bundle. Betty quickly examined the bird.

'I've already taken a look at it,' Mrs Hope confirmed. 'It's uninjured but very thin. I think it must have been the smallest of the brood.'

Betty went over to the cupboard and took out a plastic bottle. She covered the owl's face with one hand then quickly puffed a white powder into its feathers.

'That's to get rid of any vermin,' she explained.

Betty placed the owlet carefully in the cage. A cloud of white dust flew out as it shook its feathers then settled in one corner looking hunched up and miserable.

Betty perched on the edge of the desk. She looked thoughtful. 'I've had a couple of owls before,' she said. 'They both went over to Longmoor Owl Rehabilitation Centre. Once I've persuaded this one to eat properly I'll take it over there. They'll keep it for a few weeks then release it back into the wild as soon as it's fit.'

'Couldn't we do that?' asked Mandy. She felt

disappointed. She would love to have seen the owl fly safely away.

Betty shook her head. 'I'm not licensed to do that,' she explained. 'And the owl must never be handled again once it's accepting food, otherwise it'll never be able to be released. I haven't got those kind of facilities here, Mandy.'

'Why mustn't you handle it?' asked James.

'Because it will learn to rely on humans to feed it,' explained Betty.

'What will you give it?' James asked. He peered into the cage. The owl blinked slowly at him.

'Well,' Betty said thoughtfully. 'I'll have to force-feed it at first. Owls mainly eat small mammals and birds in the woodlands. In the summer they hunt more in the open and catch rabbits, moles – even earthworms.'

'I could go and dig up some worms,' said James.

'I shouldn't worry just yet, James,' Betty said. 'He won't eat anything for a while. And he couldn't have worms for long. Owls need feathers and bones in their diet. I'll try and get some chicks from the chicken farm if they'll give them to me.' She glanced at Mrs Hope. 'This could be the last creature I'm able to help, I'm afraid, Mandy. The buildings are badly in need of repair and it's going to cost at least five hundred pounds to have them done.'

'Five hundred pounds!' Mandy gasped.

'Yes,' Betty said, shaking her head. 'And to cap it all, Sam Western's put up my rent. I simply don't have enough money to pay him, do the repairs *and* feed the animals as well.'

Sam Western was a local farmer who ran his large farm like a factory. He was well-known for being both bad-tempered and mean. He was a tough businessman with no love for animals. He wouldn't care what happened to the waifs and strays at the sanctuary if it had to close.

Mandy's sadness turned to anger. 'Why has Mr Western done a mean thing like that?' she blurted.

'I think he wants the bungalow for one of his farm workers,' Betty explained. 'He knows I can't afford to pay him a higher rent.'

'But you *can't* close down, Betty,' Mandy said, almost in tears. 'The sanctuary is your life!'

'I'm sorry, Mandy,' Betty said, sounding close to tears herself. 'I really don't have any choice.'

'But what will happen to all the animals you've got here?' cried Mandy.

'I'll find homes for as many as possible,' Betty

said. 'I've been in touch with the RSPCA but they've told me they're overcrowded already. I'm afraid the rest will have to be destroyed.'

It was just as Mandy had feared. 'James and I are going to try to think of a way to get some money to help you,' she said.

'That's right,' James agreed, nodding his head like mad.

Betty sighed. 'I'm very grateful, you two, but I'm afraid it'll take more than your pocket money to save this place.'

'Oh, no,' said Mandy. 'I mean *raise* money like we do at school. We need to sit down and make a plan. Isn't that right, James?'

'Yup,' James nodded fiercely. 'We're going to do it as soon as we get back home.'

'That's very kind of you,' Betty said gratefully. 'But five hundred pounds is an awful lot of money, I'm afraid.'

'I'll give you my pocket money to help pay for the owl's food,' Mandy glanced at her mother with shining eyes. 'That'll be OK, won't it, Mum?'

Mrs Hope patted her daughter's shoulder. 'Yes, of course, Mandy, every little helps.'

'So you'll be able to keep the baby owl here for now?' Mandy asked Betty.

Betty nodded. 'Yes, I promise. I'll ring the chicken farm straight away. Perhaps you'd like to come back in a couple of days, Mandy, to see how he's getting on?'

'You bet,' said Mandy. 'I wouldn't miss it for the world. Please try to hang on, Betty. We'll think of something; I know we will!'

Mandy and James left Mrs Hope talking to Betty and wandered outside

In the paddock, Bubbles, a fat, black Shetland pony with short legs trotted up to the fence when he saw Mandy and James. Bubbles had been

rescued by Betty when his owner's children had outgrown him. He put his nose through the rails and nuzzled Mandy's sleeve. With tears in her eyes, she fondled his coarse forelock.

'I can't bear to think of it, James,' she sniffed. 'Poor old Bubbles might have to be put down.'

'I know,' James said glumly. 'No one's going to want an old pony like him. That's why he's here in the first place.'

'*I* would,' Mandy said indignantly. 'I'd love to have him.' But in her heart she knew it was impossible. There was no room at Animal Ark to keep a pony, even one as small as Bubbles.

They left Bubbles and walked between the lines of dog kennels. Some were badly in need of repair. In one, a small mongrel jumped up at the wire when it saw them coming. The dog's name, Midge, was written on a plaque by the door.

'Hello, Midge.' Mandy knelt to stroke the puppy. It wagged its tail, jumping up to try to lick her face through the wire.

Mandy stood up with a sigh. The dog whined pitifully as they walked away.

'Look,' said Mandy. 'There's old Clarence, that ram Betty saved from slaughter. And that Jersey heifer Sam Western was going to have killed because she's only got one eye.'

'No one's going to want her, either,' James said sadly. He stood on the bottom rail of the fence and scratched the heifer's poll.

'Come on,' Mandy said with another sigh. 'Let's go and sit in the car and try to think what we can do to help.'

Mrs Hope came out of the office with Betty. 'Thanks, Betty,' she said. 'We'll come up again as soon as we can.'

Mandy and James said their goodbyes and climbed into the car. Blackie greeted them with a wildly wagging tail.

Mandy patted his head absent-mindedly. There was no time to waste. If they didn't think of something to save the sanctuary *soon*, it could well be too late!

'Why don't we just go and see Mr Western?' Mandy suggested as they drove out of the gate. She turned to wave to Betty as she closed and locked the gate behind them. 'We could just ask him not to put the rent up.'

Mrs Hope shook her head. 'Don't be daft, Mandy. You know what type of man he is. He's a businessman as well as a farmer. He won't care about stray animals. They're not worth twopence to someone like him.'

Mandy sighed. 'It might be worth a *try*.'

'No, Mandy,' Mrs Hope said firmly. 'I can promise you it wouldn't.'

On the way back to Animal Ark, Mandy and James tried to come up with a way to raise money.

'We could have a jumble sale,' James suggested.

'Where would you hold it?' Mrs Hope asked.

'The village hall?' said James.

Mrs Hope glanced at them in the mirror. 'It's usually booked up ages in advance. I'm afraid Betty needs that money pretty urgently.'

Mandy pulled a thoughtful face. 'How about a sponsored swim at school, then?' she said. Then her face fell. Swimming in the school's outdoor pool at this time of year wouldn't be any fun at all. Nobody was *that* silly. No, they had to think of something else.

'A sponsored bike ride?' James piped up. 'Loads of people would do it. Your grandad for instance.'

Mandy bit her lip. 'That's not a bad idea, James. But we had one last term, remember? People might not want to do one again so quickly.'

'That's true,' James said, raising his eyebrows.

All the way home, Mandy racked her brains.

Most of her friends in the village were animal lovers. And most owned pets of one kind or another. She felt sure they would want to help. But it had to be more than just *giving* money. There were so many charities needing funds. The Reverend Hadcroft had started an appeal to repair the church roof. There was a big board by the lichgate with marks to show how much money had been raised. The marker was only up to two hundred pounds so he needed lots more before work on the roof could even begin.

Someone from the village was always calling round collecting money for charities – guide dogs for the blind, the lifeboat men. They were all very good causes. If Mandy and James were going to get money for the sanctuary it had to be something the villagers could really get involved in – something that would be fun *and* raise funds at the same time. Something that had never happened in Welford before.

As Mrs Hope drove along the village high street with its pretty green in the centre and old-fashioned shops, Mandy suddenly brightened.

'I know,' she said. 'Let's go and see Gran and Grandad. They'll help us think of something.'

'Good idea,' said James. 'Maybe your gran's

done some baking. All this thinking is making me hungry!'

Mandy's grandparents lived just up the road from Animal Ark, in a house called Lilac Cottage.

In the drive, Mandy's grandad was unloading plastic carrier bags from his new camper van. He looked delighted to see them.

'Come in and have a cup of tea!' he called.

Mrs Hope wound down her window. 'I'd love to, Dad,' she called to her father-in-law. 'But I've got a few calls to make. These two want to pick your brains.'

Grandad ran his hand through his thatch of white hair. 'What now?' he asked with a broad grin.

Mandy and James jumped out of the back. James opened the rear door for Blackie. Blackie ran up to Grandad and stuck his nose into one of the carrier bags.

'Blackie!' James shouted. He ran to grab the dog's collar.

'The animal sanctuary's going to have to close and we're trying to think of a way to save it – oh, Grandad, you've got to help us!' Mandy said all in one breath.

Grandad put his arm round her shoulders. 'Now

calm down, Mandy. Help me with these bags and we'll go and see what Gran can find us to eat. No good thinking on an empty stomach.' He waved to Mrs Hope. 'See you later, Emily.'

Mrs Hope put the car into gear and drove off down the street.

By now, Blackie had pulled out a packet of crisps. It was clamped firmly between his teeth and he was shaking it to and fro, growling. James was desperately trying to get it away from him.

'I'm ever so sorry, Mr Hope.' James went red. Trust Blackie to show him up.

'Oh, let him have it,' Mandy's grandfather said amiably. 'It can be his elevenses.'

James let go the other end of the crisp packet and it suddenly burst all over the path. Blackie ran around gobbling up crisps like a vacuum cleaner.

Laughing, Mandy and James helped Mr Hope carry the shopping indoors. They went up the garden path, under the budding lilac tree that gave the cottage its name, and in through the back door.

In the cosy kitchen, with its pine cupboards and bright red gingham curtains, Mandy's grand-mother was putting groceries away in the larder.

The kettle was already boiling on the worktop by the sink.

'Mandy, James, where did you come from?' Gran exclaimed as they all came into the kitchen. She looked delighted to see them.

Mandy put the carrier bags on the kitchen table and ran to give her grandmother a hug. She loved coming to the cottage and chatting with her grandparents. Whenever she had a problem, they always seemed to find the answers.

'What's up, Mandy?' Gran said, looking at her knowingly. She always seemed to sense when something was wrong.

Grandad came in. 'She's getting in a stew over the animal sanctuary,' he said.

Over steaming mugs of hot chocolate and a plate of home-made cookies, Mandy and James told them the full story.

'So you see,' Mandy said unhappily, 'we've got to get a move on. And at the moment we just can't think of *anything*. Can we, James?'

James shook his head, his mouth too full to speak.

Gran and Grandad looked glum.

'It's going to take a great deal of money to ensure the sanctuary stays open, Mandy,' Grandad said doubtfully. 'Those places are expensive to run.'

'I know, Grandad,' Mandy said, her eyes bright. 'Betty needs five hundred pounds to repair the buildings right away. That's why we've got to think of something really original, something everyone will want to help with.'

'I suggested a sponsored bike ride,' said James.

'Great idea!' said Mandy's grandfather. He was an enthusiastic bike rider and could often be seen pedalling in the countryside surrounding the village.

'But we had one last term,' James went on. 'Mandy said people won't want to do that again.'

'That's probably true,' said Grandad, looking serious again. He looked at his wife expectantly. 'Come on, Dorothy. You're usually full of ideas.'

Mandy's grandmother was always campaigning for something or other; writing letters to Parliament, getting up petitions. Not long ago she'd saved the village post office from being closed down. This time though, she seemed stumped.

Gran took off her glasses and laid them on the table. She rubbed her eyes. 'I know,' she said suddenly. 'How about a sponsored dog walk?'

'That's a good idea,' said James. 'Blackie would love that.'

At the word 'walk' Blackie's ears pricked up. He jumped up and put his front paws on the table. His tongue lolled out and his tail was wagging furiously.

'No, Blackie,' James said patiently. 'We're not going for a walk. Not now.' He tried to push Blackie down but the dog refused to budge. He just barked and wagged his tail harder still.

Mandy laughed. 'You'll have to stop saying that word, James.'

'Down, Blackie!' James frowned, sneaking Blackie a piece of biscuit to make sure he did as he was told.

'It's a good idea, Gran,' Mandy went on. 'But a dog would only involve people who own dogs.'

'How about a *pet* walk?' said Gran putting her glasses back on. She said the word 'walk' quietly so Blackie wouldn't hear.

Mandy giggled in spite of herself. 'Oh, Gran. I can't see anyone wanting to sponsor a tortoise! I want to get the whole village involved.'

'Well . . .' Grandad said slowly, 'how about one of those shows? You know, where you get a prize for the best rabbit, the most obedient dog – that sort of thing.' He brushed a crumb from his moustache. 'Then even people with pet spiders will be able to take part.' He sat back looking pleased with himself.

Mandy took a deep breath. What a terrific idea! Trust Grandad to come up trumps.

She jumped up from her chair and ran to give her grandfather a hug. 'Oh, Grandad, that's brilliant! We could have the best cat, the best hamster . . . even the best *rat*. We could call it the Grand Novelty Village Pet Show.'

'Well,' said her grandmother. 'That does sound *very* grand indeed.'

'It will be,' Mandy said. 'It will be the grandest event the village had ever seen. Oh, Grandad, it's perfect!'

'I've got an idea,' James said. He had been looking very thoughtful.

They all gazed at him expectantly.

'What?' asked Mandy.

'We could call our campaign SOS.'

'SOS?' asked Grandad, looking puzzled.

'Yup,' said James smugly. 'Save Our Sanctuary.'

Mandy took one last gulp of hot chocolate and slammed her mug down on the table. She ran the back of her hand across her mouth. 'Come on,

James. Let's get back to Animal Ark. I'll phone Betty to see if she thinks it's a good idea too. Then we'll start making plans!'

Three

James hurriedly finished his biscuit. He said goodbye to Mandy's grandparents and dashed after Mandy. She was already halfway down the road.

'Come *on*, James,' she called over her shoulder. 'There's no time to waste!'

When they arrived at Animal Ark, a woman dressed in old black wellington boots and a brown jacket stood on the path outside the surgery door. She was desperately hanging on to the halter of a restless black goat. The goat had perky ears and a tail that waggled about as if it were on a spring. The woman was obviously having trouble holding him. The goat's delicate hooves clattered on the path like castanets.

It was Lydia Fawcett from High Cross Farm. She owned a herd of lively goats and this one looked as if it was the liveliest of them all! But Lydia usually treated her animals with home-made remedies. She never came to the vets' unless something was seriously wrong. What on earth was she doing here?

Mandy ran up to her. 'Hello, Lydia. Can I help?' she asked, almost laughing at the goat's antics. He certainly didn't look very sick.

Lydia twisted the halter in an effort to steady him. 'Oh, yes, please, Mandy,' she said. 'Could you go in and get your father for me? Monty's got a really bad leg. I've tried to treat it myself but it's getting worse.'

Mandy stared at the goat. It was leaping about on three legs like a ballet dancer. James stood at the gate, his hand over his mouth to try to stop himself laughing. He held tightly on to Blackie's lead. If Monty broke free, there was nothing Blackie liked better than a good game of chase.

'Hang on,' Mandy said, 'I'll go and fetch someone.' She ran in through the surgery door.

Mr Hope was writing up his notes from morning

surgery. He looked up and gave a broad, lop-sided grin as Mandy rushed in. 'What's up?'

'Dad,' Mandy said urgently, 'Lydia's outside with Monty. I think you'd better go and see him before he causes havoc.'

'Lydia?' Mr Hope was already grabbing his bag. 'It must be bad if she's dragged Monty all the way to the surgery!'

Outside, Lydia was still grappling with Monty. James was standing beside her looking a bit helpless.

'Now, Lydia,' Mr Hope smiled kindly into Lydia's agitated face. 'What's wrong with Monty?'

'He's got a nasty swelling on his back leg,' Lydia said. 'I tried to treat it myself but I'm afraid it's only got worse. *Monty*!' she said angrily. 'Will you please have the good manners to stand still!' Monty ignored his mistress and went on bucking.

'Hmm,' said Mr Hope. 'Let's take a look. Try and hold him still please, Lydia.'

'I'm trying!' Lydia gasped.

Adam Hope couldn't help grinning. He turned to his daughter. 'Give Lydia a hand, will you please, Mandy.'

Mandy put her arms round the goat's neck and gripped tight. She murmured soothing words into his ear. 'Nice Monty, good Monty. Now let Dad take a look at that leg. He won't hurt you, I promise.' The goat tossed his head and rolled his eyes at her. Mandy tried her hardest to keep him steady.

Mr Hope put his bag on the ground and bent to examine one of the animal's hind legs. Then he stood up, looking serious.

'I'm afraid he's got rather a nasty abscess. He's probably been kicked by one of the other goats. Go and ask Simon for the razor and some antibiotics, please, Mandy.'

'OK, Dad.' Mandy let go Monty's neck and dashed back inside. She soon returned with the things her father wanted. Monty seemed to have calmed down a bit and was standing still, trying to eat the hedge.

'Now, hold him steady,' said Mr Hope as Monty eyed him warily. He seemed to know just what Mr Hope intended to do.

Mandy and James helped hold Monty still while Mr Hope quickly shaved the hair from round the abscess.

'Hmm . . . nasty,' Mr Hope mumbled to himself. He took the hypodermic from its sterile pack and inserted the point into a small bottle full of

antibiotic. He drew the liquid into the body of the syringe. 'Right,' he said. 'Here goes.'

He skilfully injected the goat's flank so quickly Monty hardly seemed to notice. The animal didn't flinch. 'There,' said Mr Hope, rubbing the spot where he had stuck the needle in. He stood back, looking satisfied. 'He's as good as gold.'

Then Mr Hope took a small pot from his bag. 'I'll just rub on this ointment to soothe it. There's no need to strangle him, Mandy. I'm sure he'll be fine now.'

But Mr Hope spoke too soon. As he rubbed on the ointment, Monty suddenly kicked out. Mr Hope fell back in surprise, landing in a heap on the path. Mandy and James jumped sideways as the goat took to its heels and galloped off. Lydia was still hanging on to the halter. Blackie barked excitedly, doing his best to drag James after them.

'Thank you very much, Adam!' Lydia shouted over her shoulder, her black wellingtons going like pistons.

By now, goat and owner were halfway across the village green. A line of churned-up turf showed where they had trampled across. Mandy and James collapsed into laughter.

'Are you OK, Dad?' Mandy spluttered as her

father scrambled to his feet. He brushed the dirt from the seat of his jeans.

'Great,' he said looking a bit dazed. 'I don't know what Lydia feeds her goats on – the same stuff racehorses eat I should think!'

Still laughing, all three of them went into Animal Ark. Mandy loved helping her father with his patients. It gave her a great feeling to know she'd had a hand in making them better.

They followed Mr Hope into the surgery and watched while he unpacked his bag and put the used syringe and bottle into the waste bin. He went to the sink and scrubbed his hands.

'Have you heard about Betty's sanctuary having to close?' Mandy asked, sobering up.

'Yes,' Mr Hope said grimly. 'Your mum's been telling me the sad story. Have you decided what to do?'

'Yes,' Mandy said, her eyes shining. 'We're going to have a Grand Novelty Village Pet Show. I'm just going to phone Betty and see what she thinks of the idea.'

Mr Hope raised his eyebrows. 'Well, I think it's a great idea. Where are you going to hold it?'

Mandy glanced at James. She hadn't really thought about where they would hold the show.

'On the village green, I suppose.' she said. 'And we'll need someone to judge the animals. You and Mum will do it, won't you, Dad?'

Mr Hope looked affectionately at his daughter. 'Oh, I should think we could manage that.'

'And we'll need prizes and tables and—' Mandy broke off. She began to feel worried. It had suddenly dawned on her just how much organisation was needed. But she was never one to refuse a challenge.

She jumped off the couch. 'Come on, James. Let's go and phone Betty. Then we'd better make a list of things we need to do.'

'If you're having it on the green, you'll need permission from the parish council,' Mr Hope called as they rushed out.

Mandy came back, looking anxious. 'Why?'

'Well, the green belongs to them. You can't just go holding things on it without permission.'

'OK, then,' said Mandy. 'Who do I ask?'

'Mr Markham,' Adam Hope told her. 'He's the chairman. He lives at number two, The Terrace. I went there yesterday actually – his beagle's got a litter of pups. They're a month old now and needed checking over.'

'Oh, great!' Mandy said, 'Perhaps we'll be able

to see them.' There was nothing she loved more than a litter of puppies.

'Cynthia Markham's very proud of them,' said Mr Hope. 'I'm sure she'll let you.'

Mandy and James went into the house to telephone the sanctuary. Betty answered right away.

'Oh, Mandy, I think that's a really wonderful idea,' she said when Mandy told her about the show. 'If I can do anything to help, please let me know.'

'How's the baby owl?' Mandy asked anxiously.

Betty hesitated. 'I haven't been able to get him to eat anything yet, I'm afraid. I've dug up some worms but he won't take them.'

Mandy's heart sank. 'Oh dear. Perhaps he's not hungry.'

'I think he's still in a state of shock,' Betty said. 'A fall from that height's pretty traumatic. But he's bright and beady-eyed so I'm not too worried about him. He'll soon let me know when he's hungry.'

'I'll come and see him as soon as I can,' Mandy promised.

'Any time,' Betty said. 'And let me know how plans are going for the show.'

'We will.' Mandy put the phone down with a sigh. Then she straightened up. It was pointless worrying about the owl. She knew Betty would do her best with him.

James was waiting in the hall with Blackie.

'Betty thinks the show's a brilliant idea,' Mandy told him. 'Let's go and see Mr Markham and find out if we can hold it on the green!'

The Terrace was a row of pretty Victorian cottages just off the lower high street. Number two had a green-painted front door.

Mandy went boldly up the steps and rang the doorbell.

James tied Blackie to the gate-post and went to join her.

As the door opened, a chorus of barks and yelps came from the end of the long hallway. A grey-haired woman in trousers and a long, striped cardigan stood smiling at Mandy and James.

Mandy swallowed hastily. 'Good morning,' she said with a smile. 'I'm Mandy Hope. Could we see Mr Markham, please?'

Mrs Markham knew straight away who Mandy was. 'Oh, you're the vets' daughter,' she said standing to one side. 'Come on, come in. Have you come to see my Bunty's pups?'

Mandy bit her lip. 'I'd love to,' she told Mrs Markham. 'But could we see your husband first, please? It's very important.'

'Yes, of course,' Mrs Markham said.

'Thanks,' said Mandy. 'This is my friend James Hunter.'

James held out his hand solemnly. 'How do you do,' he said.

The woman shook his hand. 'Can I ask what you want to see my husband about?'

Mandy explained about their plan to raise money for the animal sanctuary.

Mrs Markham looked impressed. 'My, you two, you *are* good. Giving up your time to help Miss Hilder.'

'It's for the sake of the animals,' Mandy said. 'They'll have to be put down and we can't bear the thought of it.'

James shook his head. 'That's right,' he said. 'Betty needs at least five hundred pounds, and we're going to get it for her.'

'My, my, you are determined,' Mrs Markham's voice was full of admiration. She patted James's head as if he were six years old. James gave her a false kind of grin. 'I'm sure my husband will help you if he can,' Mrs Markham went on. 'Come this way, children.'

Mrs Markham led Mandy and James along the carpeted hallway. Through the kitchen door, Mandy spotted a beagle in a huge dog basket feeding a row of six plump puppies. Mandy let out her breath in delight as they passed.

Mrs Markham ushered them into one of the back rooms. A tall, thin man with a bald head sat tapping away at an ancient typewriter. He turned as they entered and peered at them over the top of his spectacles.

'These young people would like to have a word with you about something, Robert,' Mrs Markham explained. 'I'll leave you to it.'

Mandy turned to say thanks but Mrs Markham had bustled away and shut the door behind her.

Mr Markham looked Mandy and James up and down with a stern expression on his face. Mandy felt as if she was standing in front of the head teacher at school.

She had seen Mr Markham before, walking through the village with a clipboard and pen, writing furiously as if he was making notes about everybody. She didn't know how old he was but he looked pretty ancient and *terribly* stern. She suddenly felt very nervous.

Mr Markham continued peering at Mandy and James over the top of his spectacles. A frown creased his shiny brow. Then, suddenly he took off his glasses and smiled. The smile seemed to change his whole face. Little blue eyes sparkled beneath his beetle-brows.

Mandy relaxed. Maybe this interview wasn't going to be so bad after all!

'Well, young people,' Mr Markham put his spectacles down on the desk. 'What can I do for you?'

Mandy explained all over again about the pet show and the animal sanctuary.

To their dismay, Mr Markham shook his head. 'I'm sorry,' he said. 'We just can't do it I'm afraid.'

Mandy tried to hide her disappointment. 'Why not?'

'It's because of that car boot sale the Young Farmers Club held at Easter time, you see.'

Mandy frowned. She didn't see at all. What had a boot sale got to do with a pet show? They weren't *selling* pets, just showing them.

'The grass got so churned up,' Mr Markham explained, 'that the parish council agreed it wouldn't let any more events be held there until next year. I'm sorry, young lady, but you'll have to find somewhere else to have your pet show. Unless you can wait until next year.'

Mandy shook her head. 'We can't. Betty Hilder needs the money *now.*'

Mr Markham shook his head again. 'Sorry. There's nothing I can do.'

He stood up and went with them to the door. 'If you do find somewhere suitable, let me know,' he said. 'I'd like to bring Bunty along. I'm sure she'd win a prize.'

'Oh, yes, please do bring her,' Mandy said enthusiastically. Trying to swallow her disappointment she led the way along the hallway towards the kitchen where Mrs Markham was giving the beagle a drink of milk. The puppies were playing on the rug, barking and tumbling and having mock battles with one another.

'Come on in,' she called to Mandy and James, who were hesitating in the doorway. It didn't seem quite polite to go barging into the room without being asked.

Mandy went in and sat down on the floor. Seeing the litter of puppies had cheered her up.

'They're absolutely gorgeous,' she said, holding

one gently up to her cheek. She felt the warm, soft fur against her skin. The puppy squirmed and tried to get a mouthful of her hair. Mandy laughed and put him down with his brothers and sisters. He ran off, his roly-poly body wobbling, and disappeared under the kitchen table.

Mrs Markham sighed. 'Yes, I'll really miss them when they have to go.'

'Have you found homes for them all?' asked James, playing tag with a puppy with a pretty brown face and floppy ears.

Mrs Markham nodded. 'Yes, I advertised them in the local paper. They were soon snapped up.'

'Not like those poor dogs at the sanctuary,' Mandy said sadly, getting up, ready to leave.

'Was my husband able to help you?' Mrs Markham said as she went with them to the front door.

Mandy shook her head sadly. 'No. He said an event like that would churn up the grass too much.'

'Oh, dear,' said Mrs Markham. 'I remember what the green looked like after that boot sale last year. It was more like a ploughed field than a village green. Did my husband have any other suggestions?'

Mandy shook her head again. 'No, not really.'

'I am sorry,' Mrs Markham said. 'Let me know if you have any luck finding somewhere else.' Then, suddenly, her face lit up. 'I know,' she said. 'Why don't you ask Amelia Ponsonby?'

'Mrs *Ponsonby*!' Mandy and James chorused.

'Yes,' said Mrs Markham. 'Do you know her?'

Mandy and James stared at each other. They had had dealings with Mrs Ponsonby before. In fact, there was hardly anyone in the village who *hadn't* had dealings with Mrs Ponsonby one way or another. The woman made it her business to know everything and everyone in Welford!

'Do we *know* her?' James chuckled. 'Everybody knows Mrs Ponsonby.'

'Well then,' said Mrs Markham. 'Why not ask her if you can have the show at her house? Bleakfell Hall is huge and it has a great big garden. I know Mrs Ponsonby's very fond of animals. And she did adopt a dog from Betty's sanctuary. She might be willing to let you hold it there.'

Mandy looked thoughtful. Maybe Mrs Markham was right. Maybe Mrs Ponsonby *would* let them hold the show at Bleakfell Hall.

But James looked dubious. 'She's a bit of a fusspot,' he said.

'Well, it's up to you,' said Mrs Markham. 'It could be worth a try.'

They said goodbye. James untied Blackie from the gate-post and they headed off towards the village green.

'Well,' said James, seeing Mandy's thoughtful face. 'Are we going to ask Mrs Ponsonby or not?'

'Yes,' Mandy said matter-of-factly. 'Remember when she adopted her little mongrel, Toby?'

'Yes,' said James.

'Well, then we know she really cares about homeless animals. Come on, let's give it a try!'

Four

Mandy and James ran down the street and across the green towards Animal Ark, Blackie at their heels. They rushed round the back to get their bikes.

Mrs Hope came to the gate. 'Where are you two off to?'

'We're going up to Bleakfell Hall to ask Mrs Ponsonby if we can hold the pet show there,' Mandy explained hastily.

'Can I leave Blackie here, please?' James asked.

Mrs Hope took hold of the Labrador's lead. 'Yes, of course. I'll put him in the kitchen.' She pulled a wry face. 'Good luck with Mrs Ponsonby – you're going to need it!'

'Thanks, Mum,' said Mandy.

'And don't be a nuisance now,' Mrs Hope called as they pedalled away. 'Mrs Ponsonby's a very busy woman!'

They cycled pell-mell through the village. Outside the post office Mrs McFarlane was talking to the postman.

'You two are in a hurry,' she called as she saw Mandy and James speeding past.

'We're on urgent business,' James called as they pedalled by.

Halfway up to Bleakfell Hall, Mandy's courage began to fail. She slowed down and waited for James to pedal alongside her.

'What do you think she'll say?' she asked, suddenly feeling they might be on a wild goose chase.

James bit his lip. 'I don't know,' he said. 'She's awfully bossy. She might not give us a chance to tell her what it's all about.'

'Yes, I know.' said Mandy. Then she thought about Betty and the animals, and drew a deep breath. 'Well,' she said, 'we're going to ask her. She won't bite our heads off, will she?'

'She might,' said James. He had always been a bit scared of Mrs Ponsonby. She was so huge and had *such* a loud voice!

Mandy laughed at his dismal face and punched him playfully on the shoulder. 'Chin up, James. Mrs Ponsonby might be a fuss-pot but she's not a monster. Come on, I'll race you.'

'If you say so,' James mumbled.

Mandy sped on ahead. She pedalled over the bridge, and through the stone gateway, then up the long gravel drive towards the imposing front door. Bleakfell Hall was a huge grey-stone Victorian mansion with tall chimneys and towers and turrets.

To Mandy's dismay, one wing was completely encased in scaffolding. Mrs Ponsonby obviously had the builders in.

Mandy skidded to a halt on the gravel.

'Oh, no,' she said disappointedly. 'Builders!'

'She won't want to be bothered with us by the looks of it,' said James, looking crestfallen.

Mandy took a deep breath. 'Well, as we've come all this way, we might as well ask anyway.' Mandy wasn't one to be easily put off.

They leaned their bikes against one of the stone pillars that flanked the front steps and went to press the old-fashioned bell-push beside the front door.

The housekeeper answered. She was a tiny woman in an apron almost to her ankles.

'Could we see Mrs Ponsonby, please?' Mandy asked politely.

'Who shall I say is calling?' asked the house-keeper.

'Er... Mandy Hope and James Hunter,' said Mandy.

'Please wait here.' The housekeeper scuttled away along a dim corridor towards the kitchen and disappeared inside muttering to herself.

After about five minutes Mrs Ponsonby came sailing down the stairs in a tweed suit and sensible shoes. She wore a green felt hat with a feather in it over her blue-rinsed hair. Mrs Ponsonby was very fond of her hats and had one to suit every occasion. In fact, Mandy couldn't remember ever having seen her in the same hat twice. Tucked under her arm was a pale-cream Pekinese dog with tiny black, boot-button eyes. Scampering behind came Toby, a little brown mongrel. He ran up to Mandy and James barking, his tail wagging furiously. He jumped up at Mandy. She bent down to stroke him.

'Hello, Toby,' she said, tickling the little dog behind the ear. 'You look well.' She was pleased to see the little dog looking so healthy. When Betty Hilder had first brought Toby to Animal Ark, he had been abandoned with a broken leg.

Mrs Ponsonby looked very surprised to see them standing there. She peered at them through the lenses of her pink spectacles.

'Who on earth let you in?' she said loudly.

'Er . . . a lady. I think she was the housekeeper,' said Mandy in a small voice. She gazed up at Mrs Ponsonby. The woman looked larger than ever, standing above Mandy, staring down at her.

Mrs Ponsonby frowned and tutted. 'That woman is hopeless, isn't she?' she said, more to the Pekinese than to Mandy and James. 'She's probably forgotten all about you already. You could have been standing here all day.' She reached the bottom stair. 'Well, what can I do for you?' she asked. 'I'm afraid I can't cope with any more dogs, Mandy.'

'Oh, no,' Mandy assured her hastily. 'It's not that. It's something else.'

'Well?' Mrs Ponsonby raised her eyebrows.

Mandy straightened up. 'We came here to ask you a favour,' she said with determination.

Mrs Ponsonby looked suspicious. 'A favour?'

'Yes,' Mandy said breathlessly. Then she quickly explained their scheme.

Mrs Ponsonby put Pandora down on the floor. The Pekinese waddled off.

'Pandora!' called Mrs Ponsonby. 'Pandora, come back!'

Toby followed the peke. They both ignored their mistress.

When Mandy had finished explaining, Mrs Ponsonby shook her head. The feather on her hat waved about just like Pandora's tail. 'I couldn't possibly let everyone run riot in my grounds.'

'They won't run riot,' James said. 'We'll have things properly organised. Mr and Mrs Hope are going to help and I'm sure my mum and dad will too.'

Mrs Ponsonby shook her head again. 'No. It's bad enough with the builders and their great boots. I'm afraid you'll have to find somewhere else. I'd like to help but it's impossible.' She looked at them not unkindly. 'I'd be pleased to enter Pandora and Toby.' She sniffed. 'Of course, they'll win every class they enter.'

Mandy sighed and tried not to look too disappointed. 'Oh well, thanks, Mrs Ponsonby.

We'll just have to find somewhere else.'

Mrs Ponsonby escorted them to the door. 'I was just going to see Mr Western about all the mud his tractors leave on the road,' she said. 'My car gets *filthy* when I drive past his place. I *could* have a word with him about Miss Hilder's rent. He's put it up, you say?'

'Yes,' Mandy said mournfully. 'And Betty can't possibly afford to pay it and have the animal shelters repaired *and* buy food as well.'

'I'll have to find out what's going on,' said Mrs Ponsonby. She liked to know everyone's business. 'Goodbye, children,' she called as they walked forlornly down the steps.

Mandy and James got on their bikes and rode slowly down the drive.

'She didn't even say sorry,' James said grumpily.

'I know,' Mandy said with a sigh. She felt really sad. Would they ever find anywhere to hold the show? 'Oh, James,' she said miserably. '*Now* what are we going to do?'

'Go home and think,' said James.

Mandy and James arrived back at Animal Ark and sat round the kitchen table drinking Cokes.

'We could ask our headmaster if we could have

the pet show at school,' James suggested hopefully.

Mandy shook her head. 'That's no good. We want the show here in the village, don't we? It's the *Welford* sanctuary. It's got to be the *Welford* show.'

James scratched his ear. 'Hey,' he said suddenly. 'What about the Parker Smythes? They've got a great big garden *and* an indoor swimming-pool – we could have dog swimming races!'

Mandy pulled a face. 'The Parker Smythes? I don't think that's a very good idea. You know how stuck-up they are.'

'Well,' said James, 'Mrs Parker Smythe loves showing off. You know she does. If we held the show there, everyone in the village would be able to see her posh house and posh swimming-pool, wouldn't they?'

'Hmm . . .' said Mandy. 'That's true. I hadn't thought of that.'

'And she loves bragging about Mr Parker Smythe being a producer on telly,' James went on. 'She could tell everyone that too.'

Mandy decided it was worth a try. She jumped up. 'OK, James. You've convinced me! Let's go and ask.'

The Parker Smythes lived in Beacon House, a

huge, white mansion set high up on Beacon Hill. It looked down on the rest of the village just as Mrs Parker Smythe looked down on its inhabitants.

Mandy and James rode up there in no time at all.

Outside the mansion's high security gates, Mandy's heart sank. The notice 'Trespassers will be prosecuted' seemed a bad omen. Maybe it had been a mistake to come here. The huge gates and the notice hardly welcomed people to the house.

Mandy sat astride her bike with her feet on the ground. She looked at James. 'What do you think?'

James shrugged and took off his glasses. He polished them on the knee of his jeans then put them back on. 'I don't know,' he said.

Mandy chewed her lip. It was really important that they got the pet show organised as soon as possible. They had got to find somewhere to have the show. This could be their very last chance.

Mandy combed her hair back with her fingers and squared her shoulders determinedly. She had made up her mind to give it a try.

'Well,' she said to James. 'Here goes!'

She stood on tiptoe and pressed a button on the security intercom attached to one of the pillars. There was a hiss and a popping noise and a squeaky voice asked who was there.

Mandy told the machine and after another click the huge gates swung silently open. It was like getting permission to enter a prison!

Mandy and James cycled along the drive, through the little spinney and between neat hedges that led up to the front door. Their ring on the bell was answered straight away.

A short, overweight girl stood dwarfed by the huge door frame. She was dressed in bright pink Lycra leggings and a white fluffy jumper with a kitten embroider on the front. She had chocolate all round her mouth.

'Yes?' she asked. 'Have you come to play with me?' Her tongue came out as she tried to lick the chocolate off.

'Hi, Imogen,' Mandy said brightly. Imogen was the spoiled seven-year-old daughter of the Parker Smythes.

'Is your mum in?' James piped up.

'She's in the sauna,' said Imogen, as if taking a sauna was the most ordinary thing in the world.

'A sauna!' James spluttered beside Mandy.

Mandy nudged him. There was only one way to deal with Imogen and that was to be as sweet as pie.

'Any idea how long she'll be?' she asked the little girl gently.

Imogen wriggled around as if she had a scorpion in her knickers. 'Yes,' she said. 'Ages probably. She and Daddy went to a party last night and Mummy's recovering.'

'Oh,' said Mandy, not knowing quite what else to say.

'But come in and play with me,' Imogen insisted. 'Daddy's bought me a new doll's-house and I've got a new video and lots of—'

Just then Mrs Parker Smythe came through into the hallway. Mandy sighed with relief. She'd thought Imogen would never stop.

Mrs Parker Smythe was swathed from head to immaculately painted scarlet toenail in a pure white, fluffy, towelling robe. Her blonde hair was covered by a peach coloured turban.

'Who is it, Immie darling?' she enquired.

'Mandy Hope and James Hunter,' Imogen replied. 'They've come to play with me.'

'Er . . . no,' Mandy said. 'Sorry, we actually wanted to see your mum.'

Imogen stuck out her bottom lip in a sulk. 'It's not fair,' she moaned. 'No one ever comes to play with me.'

'I'm not surprised,' James whispered to Mandy.

Mrs Parker Smythe tottered towards them across the marble floor. She wore white satin high-heeled mules that slipped and slithered as if the floor was covered with ice.

She stared at Mandy. 'You're the vets' daughter, aren't you?'

'Yes,' Mandy confirmed. She went on talking quickly. She knew if she let Mrs Parker Smythe get a word in edgeways she would hear grand tales of her husband's involvement in television, the famous people that came to stay in Beacon House and stories of how brilliant dear Immie was at all kinds of things from playing the piano to tap-dancing.

When Mandy finished telling Mrs Parker Smythe why they were there, the woman sat down heavily on one of the gold brocade chaise-longues that lined the sparkling hallway.

'I'm not sure my husband would relish the idea of the hoi polloi coming up here in droves,' she said.

'What's hoi polloi?' James whispered in Mandy's ear.

'No idea,' Mandy whispered back.

Mrs Parker Smythe looked at them as if they

were something that had crawled from the woodwork. 'Hoi polloi,' she said, obviously overhearing. 'Villagers . . . you know, *common* people.'

'But you would love them to see your gorgeous house, wouldn't you?' said Mandy. 'And your lovely garden. Your husband could even make a film of the event.' She turned to Imogen, 'You could be the star, Imogen.'

Imogen began to jump up and down waving her fat fists in the air. 'Yes Mummy, yes Mummy, yes Mummy,' she chanted.

Mrs Parker Smythe passed her hand across her eyes. 'Immie darling, I've got the most dreadful headache.' She looked slightly bewildered.

Imogen ran up to her and banged her on the knee. 'I want the pet show here!' she shouted. 'I want to be a film star!'

Mandy glanced at James and could see he was tempted to throw darling Immie into the Parker Smythes' posh indoor swimming-pool.

Mrs Parker Smythe was trying to calm her daughter down. 'Very well, dear,' she was saying. 'We'll have a little pet show if that's what you want.' She glanced up at Mandy and James. 'But it will have to be dear little bunnies and kittens and

things like that. I can't have great big dogs
trampling over my beautiful Persian rugs.'

'The animals wouldn't have to come indoors,'
Mandy assured her.

Mrs Parker Smythe waved her hand. 'Well, they
might make messes on the lawn. We've got the
famous Italian film director Mario Ponti coming
next week. Can you imagine him treading . . .' She
shuddered. 'I couldn't take the risk. Just bunnies
and kitties.'

'And mice?' James asked innocently.

Mandy almost laughed out loud. At the mention
of the word 'mice' Mrs Parker Smythe gave a little
scream. Her turban wobbled and slipped to one
side. 'Mice! You aren't serious?'

Mandy couldn't resist taking it further. 'Oh, yes,'
she said. 'If it's only to be *small* pets, there'll be
mice, gerbils, spiders, rats . . .'

For one minute Mandy thought Mrs Parker
Smythe was going to faint. She went almost as pale
as her robe. They'd blown their chances of holding
the pet show at Beacon House, that was for sure!

Mrs Parker Smythe stood up shakily and took
hold of Mandy and James's elbows. She steered
them quickly to the front door. 'No, I'm sorry,'
she breathed. 'I think perhaps you'd better find

somewhere else to have your pet show. I'd be quite happy to give a donation to the sanctuary.' She shuddered again. 'But mice . . . and *rats* . . . oh dear, I feel quite faint. I think I'll go and have a lie-down.'

She pushed Mandy and James through the door and shut it firmly behind them. In the hall, Imogen began to shout and scream, 'I want mice, I want mice, I want mice!'

James took the lead. He grabbed Mandy's arm. 'Come on, let's go.'

Still giggling they tore off down the drive. The huge gates opened as if by magic and they were through, pedalling back down the hill towards the village. Mandy threw back her head and laughed. Mrs Parker Smythe's expression when they mentioned the mice had been a picture!

'Did you see her face?' Mandy chortled. 'Oh dear, poor Mrs Parker Smythe, she'll have nightmares for a week. Whose idea was it to go there, James?'

'Mine,' James said sheepishly. 'Sorry.'

Mandy stopped her bike and looked at the wide sweeps of moorland, and the blue sky with just a few cotton-wool clouds drifting slowly across the tops of the hills. She heaved a sigh. She felt disappointed. But holding a pet show at Beacon House would never have worked. They'd just have to find somewhere else.

'It's OK, James,' she said. 'We're not giving up yet. Come on. Let's get back and see what other bright ideas we can come up with, shall we?'

When they reached the village, James went into the post office to get some sherbet lemons while Mandy waited outside. When James came out, they parked their bikes by the village seat and sat down. The village seat was always a good place to sit and think. Mandy's mind was racing. They'd tried three things now and nothing was working out. She began to feel desperate. Someone, somewhere, must be willing to host the show.

The Reverend Hadcroft came cycling down the road on his old black bicycle. He went into the post office and came out with the daily paper under his arm.

'Hello, you two,' he called. 'You look down in the dumps.'

'We are,' James called.

The vicar strolled over and sat beside them. He was a young man with a shock of black hair and bright blue eyes.

'OK,' he said. 'Tell me what's up.'

Between them they told him their story.

Mr Hadcroft frowned and fiddled thoughtfully with the edge of his cassock. 'It seems to me,' he said wisely, 'that you two are making a mountain out of a molehill.'

A mountain out of a molehill! Mandy thought indignantly. Saving the animal sanctuary was just about the most important thing in the world right at that moment!

'What do you mean?' she asked, puzzled.

The vicar grinned broadly. 'Well,' he said, 'why not hold it in the vicarage garden? If it's good enough for the Women's Institute to hold their summer fête, then it's good enough for you to hold a pet show, isn't it?'

Mandy's heart leaped. The vicarage garden would be excellent! It had a big square lawn with lots of places to put tables and mark out parade rings. It would be just brilliant!

'Oh, wow, Mr Hadcroft,' she said excitedly. 'Could we?'

Mr Hadcroft grinned. 'Yes, why not?'

Mandy leapt to her feet. 'Oh, that would be really great. Thanks, Mr Hadcroft.' She felt like hugging him but wasn't quite sure if it would be the right thing to do. She turned to James, her eyes shining.

'Come on, James. There's lots to do.' They were going to have an incredibly busy half-term holiday, that was for sure!

There was a twinkle in the vicar's eye as he stood up with them. 'Of course,' he said, 'I'll need a donation for the church roof fund if I'm going to let you use my garden.'

Mandy's face fell. She knew how badly the church needed a new roof, but animals needed roofs over their heads too. 'Oh . . .' she said, trying not to sound too glum. She winced. 'How much?'

The vicar clasped his hands together in front of him and raised his eyes to the sky as if he was asking for guidance. Finally he looked at Mandy and James.

'Shall we say one pound? Could you manage that?'

Mandy stared at him. Then a huge grin broke over her face. Mr Hadcroft was as bad as her dad for teasing!

She beamed him a smile. 'I'm sure we could manage a pound, aren't you, James?'

'Absolutely,' said James.

'Great!' exclaimed Mr Hadcroft. 'You'd better come and see me later when you've made some more plans. I'll do anything to help you, of course.'

'We will,' Mandy called as they pushed their bikes hurriedly towards Animal Ark. All of a sudden she felt wonderful. She might have known they would succeed in finding somewhere. In a village like Welford there was always *someone* to lend a helping hand.

Mandy's mind was already whirling, planning their next move. She wanted to make the Grand Novelty Village Pet Show an event that no one would ever forget!

Five

Mandy and James dashed excitedly back towards Animal Ark to tell the Hopes the good news. Mandy was already thinking up ideas. They'd need tables, prizes, someone to—

Suddenly a green car swung round the corner. At the same time, it seemed from out of nowhere, a beautiful tan and black German Shepherd streaked across the green. It careered straight into the road. There was nothing the car driver could do to avoid it. There was a loud, ominous screech of brakes and a sickening thud as the front bumper hit the dog.

Mandy skidded to a halt and dropped her bike.

Her hands flew to her mouth. For a moment she froze in horror.

'Oh, no!'

Heart thudding with fear, Mandy sprang forward. The dog was lying motionless on its side in the road. The driver, a woman in her twenties, had got out and was standing looking at it, shaking her head. Tears were running down her face. She wrung her hands together in despair.

'She just ran out. There was nothing I could do!' the woman wailed.

'I know,' Mandy gasped. 'I saw her. Don't worry. It wasn't your fault.'

The young woman looked at Mandy with an agonised face. She knelt down beside the unconscious dog. 'What on earth shall we do?'

Then a young man in a black leather jacket appeared from round the corner. He had longish, thick, blond hair and a tanned face with startling blue eyes. 'Sheba!' he shouted desperately. 'Sheba!'

His eyes widened in horror when he saw what had happened.

He rushed over and knelt down beside Mandy. He rocked backwards and forwards on his heels. There were tears in his eyes as he glanced at her.

'She ran away from me,' he said, looking distraught.

'I'm so sorry,' the young woman said, wiping her eyes. 'I couldn't avoid her. She just ran out.'

'I saw it all,' Mandy said quickly. 'It couldn't be helped.'

The young man stretched his hand to touch the dog.

'No, don't touch her!' Mandy said hastily. Her mind was racing. The dog was still breathing, but unconscious. There was no sign of any blood but it would be a mistake to touch or move Sheba until either Mr or Mrs Hope had taken a look at her.

Mandy quickly shrugged off her jacket. She laid it very gently over the animal. 'I'll get help.' She turned to James. 'Don't let anyone move her,' she said urgently.

Then she was off, racing towards Animal Ark, her heart pounding. She knew the rules of first aid. Keep the animal warm, look for signs of bleeding, of broken limbs. But her mum or dad were the ones to help. People who didn't know what they were up to might do more harm than good.

Mandy flew in the surgery door. It hit the wall with a bang.

Jean Knox was just about to protest when she saw Mandy's white face.

'Where's Mum or Dad?' Mandy cried.

'In the house . . .' Jean began. But Mandy had already disappeared. She dashed through the surgery and into the kitchen.

Mr Hope was ironing his white surgery coat. He looked up in surprise as Mandy ran in.

'Quick, Dad. A dog's been knocked down!'

Mr Hope quickly switched off the iron and ran to get a blanket and his bag. He sped down the path after Mandy.

In the road, James was standing with his arms out to warn any oncoming traffic. For once, Blackie sat obediently by his feet. The young man was talking to James.

'My uncle will kill me!' he said. He sat on the kerb with his head in his hands.

'Your uncle?' asked James, waving a motorcyclist past.

'Yes, I'm staying with him at Moon Cottage. Sheba's his dog. I begged him to let me take her out. I love dogs but I live in the city and you can't keep a dog in a flat.'

Mandy arrived just in time to hear him explaining. Her heart lurched with sympathy. She knew how hard it was to control a dog like a German Shepherd if you weren't used to them.

The young man looked up. Relief crossed his face when he saw Mr Hope's leather bag.

'This is my dad,' explained Mandy, 'He's a vet. Sheba will be OK now, don't worry.'

But Mandy sounded more confident than she felt. The dog was still unconscious and her breathing was shallow. One hind leg lay at a crooked angle. Mandy could only pray it wasn't broken. Then, horrified, she noticed blood seeping from Sheba's lower jaw. Her stomach turned over. 'Dad!' she cried. 'Look!'

Mr Hope's face was grim as he knelt down beside the unconscious animal. He took out his stethoscope and listened to the dog's heart and lungs.

'They seem OK,' he said, sounding relieved. He replaced the stethoscope then gently lifted the dog's upper lip and pressed a finger against her gum. When he took it away, the gum immediately went pink again although his finger was covered in blood.

Mr Hope looked up. 'If the gum hadn't gone pink,' he explained, 'it would have meant she had internal bleeding. Luckily that seems OK. The blood's just where her teeth have pierced her lip.' He pulled the dog's eyelids open and looked into her pupils. 'She's definitely in shock. Let's hope that's all.'

He quickly examined the dog's limbs. 'Umm,' he muttered, touching the crooked hind leg. 'I spoke too soon. This one's broken, I'm afraid. Let's get her back to the surgery before she wakes up.'

Mandy helped her dad spread the blanket out on the tarmac.

'Help me,' Mr Hope said to the young man. 'And be careful,' he warned. 'If she comes round, she might bite.'

Gently supporting the dog's head and body, they lifted her on to the blanket to use it as a make-shift stretcher. Mr Hope made sure the dog's neck was extended so her breathing wasn't obstructed.

Mandy and James trailed behind as Mr Hope and the young man carried Sheba over to Animal Ark.

'Poor Sheba,' James said mournfully.

'If it's just a broken leg, she'll be OK,' said Mandy. 'Dad'll plaster it up then keep her at the Ark to make sure there's nothing worse wrong with her.'

Back at Animal Ark, Mandy and James sat in

the waiting-room with the young man. In the surgery, Mr Hope and Simon gave Sheba a more thorough examination and put her leg into plaster.

The young man introduced himself. 'I'm Mark Boston,' he said. 'I'm looking for a house to buy in Welford. It's such a great place.' He shook his head. 'I don't know if my uncle will want me living near him after this.'

Mandy tried to cheer him up. 'It really wasn't your fault,' she insisted. She suddenly realised she hadn't seen the car driver since she had rushed to get her dad. 'What happened to the woman driving the car?'

'She had to meet her kids from school,' Mark explained. 'She said she'd call in later to see how Sheba was. She felt terrible.'

'So did I,' James piped up. 'I thought Sheba was dead.'

'Don't even think about it!' Mark shook his head. He turned to Mandy. 'I don't know what I'd have done without your help, Mandy. I'm really grateful.'

Mandy shrugged. 'It's a good job we were there,' she said, 'I'd have done the same for any animal.' Her face lit up. 'I want to be a vet too.'

'Well, I'm sure you'll make a great one.'

Just then, Mr Hope came through, drying his hands on a towel.

Mark jumped up anxiously. Mr Hope put a reassuring hand on his arm. 'Now, don't panic. She's going to be OK.'

Mandy felt relief wash over her. Mark looked relieved too. He sat back down heavily. Colour flooded back into his cheeks. 'Is it just her leg?'

'I'm pretty sure that's all that's wrong with her, but I'll keep her under observation. You'd better go and tell your uncle what's happened.'

Mark pulled a worried face. 'He's going to kill me,' he repeated. 'I know he is.'

We'll come with you if you like,' volunteered Mandy. 'We can tell him it wasn't your fault.'

Mark smiled down at her. 'The thing is, Mandy, it *was* my fault. I should have had her on a lead.' He sighed. 'No, I've got to face the music.' Then he laughed loudly although Mandy couldn't quite see what was so funny.

Mark went on. 'If I do come to live near here,' he said, 'I want a house with lots of land so I can keep some animals. You two will have to come and give me a few hints on how to look after them.'

'We'd love to,' Mandy said. She liked Mark a lot.

Anyone who was fond of animals was OK in Mandy's book. And, it was very strange, she had the feeling that she'd seen Mark somewhere before.

'Excellent,' James said with a grin. He patted Blackie. 'You can practise on Blackie if you like.'

Mark smiled. 'I think I'd better have a few lessons first.'

'Have you been to Welford before?' Mandy asked. She was still puzzling over where she might have seen him.

Mark nodded. 'Years ago, when I was a kid about your age. I never forgot what a great place it was. I always had this dream of living in the country, and now I've got the money to do just that.'

They went through to see Sheba. She was awake now, sitting on the floor, licking her newly-plastered leg. She looked groggy and very sorry for herself.

'I've given her a sedative,' said Mr Hope. 'She's bound to be bruised and sore. We'll put her out in the recovery room.'

'Will she try to get the plaster off?' asked Mark.

'She might,' said Mr Hope. 'If she carries on worrying at it, we'll have to put a plastic cone over her head so she can't get at it. Let's see how she gets on first. Some dogs accept the plaster in no time at all and hop around as if they've worn it all their lives.'

Mark crouched down and fondled Sheba's head. She managed a feeble wag of her tail.

'I'm sorry, old girl,' Mark said, his voice breaking. After a minute or two he stood up, squaring his broad shoulders. 'I expect Clive, my uncle, will want to come and see her. Is that OK?'

'Of course,' said Mr Hope. 'And it'll probably be OK to pick her up this time tomorrow.'

Mark shook his hand. 'Thanks, I'm really grateful.'

'Just part of the job,' Mr Hope said. 'It's lucky

Mandy was there. If anyone had tried to move Sheba it could have caused more injury.'

'I know,' Mark said. He put his arm round Mandy and gave her a hug. 'I'll buy you a Coke sometime, Mandy, and you, James.'

Mr Hope went out with Mark, discussing fees. 'I'll pay, of course,' Mark was saying.

Mandy stood watching. Then a frown creased her brow. She chewed her lip. 'You know, James,' she said thoughtfully. 'I've seen Mark somewhere before.'

'If he came to stay in the village you might have seen him then,' James suggested.

'Maybe,' said Mandy. 'But I'd only have been a little kid. No, I've seen him recently but I just can't think where!'

When the excitement and worry of the injured dog was over, Mandy and James sat at the kitchen table with pencil and paper, making plans for the Grand Novelty Village Pet Show.

'We'll need to make some notices,' said James. He was good at that kind of thing.

'Yes,' Mandy agreed. It was vital that as many people as possible knew when and where the show would be held.

'But when *are* we going to have it?' asked James. 'We haven't decided yet.'

'Saturday's best,' said Mandy. 'When people are home from work.'

'Right,' said James. 'Next Saturday?'

'Yes,' she said quickly. 'Let's make it next Saturday!'

'We'd better ask Mr Hadcroft if that day's OK,' said James.

'Good idea,' Mandy jumped up. 'I'll phone him now.'

She came back smiling. 'Saturday's fine,' she said. 'Mr Hadcroft wondered if we'd have everything organised in time but I said we would.'

'Great,' said James. 'Right, let's make that list. First we'll need prizes.'

Mandy gulped. 'Prizes! Of course. Where are we going to get those from?'

James bit the end of his pencil. 'Um . . . I don't know.'

'I could ask Walter Pickard. He loves animals. He might find something we could give as a prize.'

'Right,' James scribbled away. 'We could just walk round the village and ask people them if they'll donate a prize. Does that sound like a good idea?'

'Brilliant,' said Mandy. 'I'm sure there's lots of people who'd give something.'

'Right,' said James. 'Now we need to decide what competitions we're going to have. Then we'll need tables, and cages and judges and a loudspeaker and . . .'

Mandy stared at him. Tables, cages . . . It looked as if finding the venue and prizes were only the first of a long line of problems they had to solve.

The door opened and Simon came through to put the kettle on. 'What's this?' he asked, peering over James's shoulder.

'A list of stuff we need for our pet show,' said James.

'You haven't got "marquee" on it,' said Simon.

Mandy gulped. 'What do we need a marquee for?'

'In case it rains, of course. You can't trust the weather this time of year. You can't parade animals round in the pouring rain. They'll end up looking like drowned rats.'

Mandy's face fell. Simon was right. She hadn't thought of that. Where on earth were they going to get a marquee from?

'The scouts have got one!' James said suddenly.

'Maybe they'd let us borrow it.'

'It would cost you,' said Simon, putting some tea into the pot. 'Loads of money.'

Mandy looked at him sideways. She had already promised her pocket money to Betty for the owl's food. Where on earth was she going to get the money to hire a marquee? Then she noticed Simon was grinning. 'You're joking, aren't you?'

'Well, maybe not loads of money but they do charge to hire it out.'

Mandy sighed. This was all becoming very complicated. But she wasn't going to be put off. Gran always said nothing was worth doing unless it was worth doing well.

'Anyway,' Simon was waiting for the tea to brew, 'why don't you ask Jean? She's friends with Mrs Browne, the scout leader. She might put in a good word for you.'

'Great, thanks, Simon. If she's Jean's friend she might let us have it for nothing!' Mandy was going to jump up to ask Jean that very minute but James held her arm.

'Hang on,' he said. 'Let's get this list done.'

Mandy sat down again. 'OK – what next?'

'The competitions.'

Mandy raised her eyebrows thoughtfully. 'Right . . . er, how about the dog with the waggiest tail?'

Simon was just pouring out mugs of tea for himself and Jean. He laughed when he heard Mandy's suggestion.

'I reckon Blackie would win that,' Simon said. He picked up the mugs and walked towards the door. 'You've got to give everyone a fair chance, you know. No favouritism.'

'We will,' Mandy said indignantly. 'That's why we're having all kinds of different classes.'

'How about the cat with the longest whiskers, then,' Simon suggested.

James scribbled away. 'Great. What else?'

'I'm sure you two will think of something.' Simon said. He pushed the door open with his foot. 'If you need any more suggestions, let me know.'

'Thanks, Simon,' Mandy said. She was still racking her brains. What kind of pets did her village friends have?

There were cats and dogs of course. Old Ernie Bell who lived near Mr Pickard had a pet squirrel. There were rabbits and guinea-pigs and she knew of at least two of her school friends who kept rats as pets. Mandy chuckled. She only had to think of the word 'rat' and she could see the chocolate-covered Imogen Parker Smythe and her poor mother's expression of horror.

There were bound to be other pets as well. Pets like budgies, parrots, stick insects, goldfish. The list was endless.

'How about the rodent with the twitchiest nose,' she suggested to James. 'That'll cover gerbils, hamsters, mice and *rats*!'

'*Rats*!' James screeched, imitating Mrs Parker Smythe, 'Oh, no, not *rats*!'

Mandy laughed. 'What else can you think of? We're not getting very far.'

'How about the most disobedient dog?' he suggested, pushing his glasses back up his nose.

'You're thinking of Blackie again,' said Mandy.

James looked indignant. 'No, I'm not. What about Pandora and Toby? Did you see the way they ignored Mrs Ponsonby this morning?'

Mandy grinned. 'I certainly did. Those dogs are wonderful at ignoring Mrs Ponsonby. They're the only ones who can!'

James laughed. 'Shall I put that on the list, then?'

Mandy nodded. 'Sure, yes, go ahead. It'll be

much more fun than the most *obedient* one. And that's what we want – people to have . . . fun!'

James was scribbling with fury. 'What else? We need about ten in all.'

'The most talkative budgie?' suggested Mandy.

'Excellent,' said James, adjusting his glasses again.

'Right,' Mandy looked thoughtful. 'Hmm . . .'

'The stickiest stick insect?' James suggested.

'Now you *are* being silly,' Mandy laughed.

The list was growing rapidly – the best rescued dog or cat, the best turned-out pet, the most unusual pet.

'My friend at school's got a pet woodlouse,' said James. 'I bet that would win.'

To round it off they decided on the dog who can eat his dinner fastest and the most scruffy pet in Welford.

They sat back looking pleased with themselves.

'Now,' said Mandy. 'The prizes.'

'And someone to present them,' added James.

Mandy bit her lip. She'd forgotten all about that. What they needed was someone famous. Someone who would really draw the crowds. Who on earth could they find? Suddenly, she had an idea. 'What about Susan Collins's mum?'

Susan and Mrs Collins lived in a big house on the road to Walton. Mrs Collins used to act in *Parson's Close*, a soap opera on TV, and still did a little acting from time to time. Her professional name was Miranda Jones.

James's eyes lit up. 'Brilliant! Give her a ring!'

She hurried out into the hall to use the phone. Minutes later, she came back looking crestfallen.

'She said she'd love to but she's got to visit her aunt in hospital on Saturday.'

James stuck his elbows on the table. 'Never mind,' he said. 'Maybe we'll think of someone else. I'll go home now and do the notices. Then we'll take them round the village tomorrow and ask people about prizes.'

'Good idea,' said Mandy. 'I can't wait!'

Six

Just as James was going out, there was a knock at the back door.

When Mandy opened it, a tall man with black hair and a beard stood on the step. He looked very upright and rather stern but when he spoke he had a kind and gentle voice. He wore jeans and an open-necked shirt with a bright scarf tied at the collar.

Although he was a relative newcomer to the village Mandy had seen the man several times before. He was a painter and he often sat down by the river with his brushes and easel, or on the village green painting watercolour pictures of the houses and church.

'My name is Clive Moon,' he said, sounding most apologetic. 'I'm sorry, the surgery seems to be closed but I wondered if I might see my dog? He was knocked down by a car when my nephew was taking him for a walk.'

'Oh, yes, please come in. I'll take you through to the recovery room,' said Mandy. 'I'm afraid the surgery doesn't open until six, except for emergencies.' She waved goodbye to James then took Mr Moon through. Simon was there, checking up on Sheba.

Mr Moon put out his hand. 'How do you do, young man. Is my dog going to be all right?' he asked Simon anxiously. He bent to caress the sleeping dog.

'Yes, she's going to be fine,' Simon reassured him. 'She'll be stiff for a while, of course. And she'll have to get used to walking on three legs while she's in plaster but it's amazing how adaptable dogs can be.'

'Is Mark OK?' Mandy asked. 'He was really upset.'

Mr Moon looked up at her then got to his feet. 'Yes, he's recovered now. I know it wasn't his fault. People drive far too fast through this village. One day someone's going to get killed. Were you the young lady who ran for the vet?'

Mandy nodded, feeling a little shy. 'He's my dad.'

'Yes, so I gather.' Mr Moon put out his hand for her to shake. 'I wanted to thank you. Mark said if it hadn't been for you, Sheba might have perished.'

Mandy almost giggled. Mr Moon made Sheba sound like an old balloon. But instead she blushed and couldn't think of anything to say.

'She's brilliant with animals,' said Simon.

'Yes.' Mr Moon gazed at Mandy. He had piercing eyes that seemed to look right through her. 'I can see that. You will make a good vet yourself one day, young lady.'

'That's what I want to be,' Mandy said, losing her shyness. Mr Moon was very friendly in a funny, old-fashioned kind of way.

'Well, I wish you good luck,' said Mr Moon. He took another look at Sheba, then Mandy saw him out.

'Dad will let you know when it's OK for her to go home,' she said.

'Goodbye, young lady,' he said. 'I look forward to seeing you again.' His funny, formal way of speaking made Mandy smile.

Mr Moon strode off down the path. He stopped by the gate to smell one of the blossoms on the rhododendron by the gate. He examined it closely then went off muttering to himself.

Mandy went back to Animal Ark to do her chores before tea. What an exciting day it had been. She swept the floor and tidied up – putting empty polythene wrappers into the bin, filling up the disposable towel holder. She sprayed disinfectant on all the surfaces and wiped them dry.

Going outside to feed her rabbits, Mandy thought again about Mark Boston. She wished she had asked his uncle where she might have seen him before. It had been puzzling her all afternoon. Maybe in the morning she would remember.

But when Mandy awoke the next day she *still* couldn't think where she'd seen Mark before. She lay in bed, staring at the animal posters on the wall. Then she suddenly remembered all the work that had to be done to organise the show. She leapt out of bed, had a quick shower and dressed in her usual jeans, trainers and sweat-shirt.

She had just finished breakfast when Mr Hope came in to ask Mandy if she'd like to help him take Sheba home. 'Then I've just got time to take you to the sanctuary to see your owl before I do my rounds,' he said.

'Thanks, Dad!' Mandy ran the tap hastily over her empty cereal bowl and left it to drain. She dashed out after him.

In the recovery room, Sheba stood on three wobbly legs drinking a bowl of milk. She wagged her tail when Mandy appeared. Mandy felt relieved to see the dog looking better. Nevertheless, her heart still skipped with pity. No matter how hard she tried she could never get used to seeing animals in pain.

She bent down to stroke the dog's head. Sheba whined then gave her a milky lick on the cheek.

'I've given her a pain-killer,' Mr Hope said. 'And I'll call and see her later to check her over.'

'Can she walk?' Mandy asked.

Mr Hope shook his head. 'She'd probably try, she's a very brave animal. But we'd better carry her to the car, she's still fairly groggy.'

Between them, Mandy and her dad carried the huge dog carefully out to the car. Mr Hope had already laid a blanket in the back.

They settled Sheba down and Mandy climbed in with her.

'Good girl,' she murmured comfortingly. 'You'll soon be home.'

Mandy stroked Sheba gently and whispered soft words of reassurance as Mr Hope drove slowly along the street and up one of the narrow alleyways that led to Mr Moon's house. It was called Moon Cottage and was one of a terrace of three stone houses with black tiled roofs and small, mullioned windows. There was a painting of a half moon below the crescent-shaped door knocker.

Mr Moon was looking anxiously out of the window. He disappeared as the car drew up outside, then the front door opened and he came out and ran to the gate.

Mandy climbed out of the back as Mr Hope came to lift Sheba out.

The dog's tail wagged joyfully and she licked his face all over as Mr Moon bent to stroke her. Mandy swallowed back tears. It was always great to see animals reunited with their owners.

Mr Moon helped Mr Hope carry the dog indoors.

'Put her on the sofa,' he said, shouting above the sound of loud pop music from a radio playing upstairs.

They settled Sheba down on the red rug that

covered the sofa. Mr Moon closed a door so they could hear themselves speak.

'She still looks a bit dazed,' he said anxiously. He sat down next to Sheba and stroked her ears.

'Yes,' said Mr Hope. 'She'll be groggy for a while.' He handed Mr Moon a bottle of tablets. 'Give her one of these three times a day,' he said. 'They'll control her pain. I'll pop in again later to see how she's doing.'

'Thank you so much,' said Mr Moon. 'I'm very grateful for what you have done.'

Mandy looked round the room. The walls were covered with Mr Moon's watercolours. There was one of Stony Bridge and another of Monkton Spinney knee-deep in bluebells like a wonderful, azure carpet. It was so lifelike Mandy could almost smell their perfume.

'Do you like my pictures?' Mr Moon asked when he saw Mandy gazing at them.

'Yes, they're lovely,' Mandy said enthusiastically. 'My friend James is good at art. I'm hopeless.'

'Well, you have other talents,' Mr Moon said, his eyes twinkling at her. 'We all have different things we can do well. Perhaps you would like to see my studio?'

'I'd love to,' said Mandy.

'If you want to see that owl of yours I'm afraid we'll have to get going,' Mr Hope said, looking at his watch.

Mandy shrugged. 'Sorry, Mr Moon. I'll come back another time if that's OK.'

'Any time you're passing,' Mr Moon assured her. He saw them out.

Halfway along the village street Mandy let out an exclamation of dismay.

'What's up?' her father asked.

'I meant to ask Mr Moon about Mark,' she said.

'What about Mark?'

'Well, I know I've seen him somewhere before and I can't think where. I thought maybe his uncle might know.'

'You'll have to ask him next time you see him,' Mr Hope said.

It was a lovely, warm, spring day as they drove the few miles to the sanctuary. When they got there, Mr Hope stopped by the gate and hooted the car horn. Betty came running out.

'We've come to see the owl,' Mandy explained as Betty unlocked the gate to let them through.

'He's still in the office,' said Betty, nodding to Mr Hope. 'Come on in, both of you.'

The owl was sitting on the perch in his hospital

cage. Mandy approached cautiously. She didn't want to frighten him. His plumage looked less ruffled than before. His broad, speckled wings were folded against his tiny body. His large feet were spread out to give him balance on the narrow perch. He looked so sweet and funny, Mandy couldn't help smiling.

'He looks better,' Mandy said, turning to the others with shining eyes.

'Yes,' said Betty. 'I've managed to persuade him to eat some earthworms and he's perked up a bit. I'm going to put him into a flight cage later.'

'What's that?' Mandy asked.

'It's a much bigger pen, out of doors,' Betty explained. 'The kind he'll be in over at the rehabilitation centre. It'll give him a chance to get used to being out in the open. So far his only experience of the outside world is his fall from the tree!'

'Poor little thing,' Mandy said softly.

'He needs room to stretch,' said Mr Hope. 'And try to use those wings of his.'

'That's right,' said Betty. 'If he doesn't he'll become very weak. He needs all his strength to learn to fly.'

'How will you get him to do that?' asked Mandy.

'They'll do it over at Longmoor,' Betty said. 'I won't keep him here much longer. He's getting too used to humans and that's not good.'

Mandy's heart went out to the little creature. It was true he looked better, more perky. But he still looked lost and lonely and she felt desperately sorry for him, especially because it was her own fault the owl was there. Owls should be out in the woods and fields, flying free, not hunched up in a cage in someone's office.

She let out a sigh and turned away. 'The sooner he's free, the better,' she said.

Betty put an arm round her shoulder. 'Mandy,

don't feel so bad. If it wasn't for you, he might be dead by now.'

'That's true,' Mandy said. But she still wasn't certain she'd done the right thing.

'Tell Betty quickly about the show, then we've got to be off,' Mr Hope told her.

Betty looked overjoyed when she heard how things were going. 'Thanks, Mandy,' she said giving her a hug. 'I did wonder if you'd like me to bring my display of the work I do here. I've got photographs and information about stray dogs and cats, that kind of thing.'

'That would be super,' Mandy said. 'Then people can see what will be done with the money we raise.'

'And let me know if I can be of any help,' said Betty.

'They seem to be getting on pretty well on their own,' Mr Hope said with a twinkle in his eye. 'You know what Mandy's like once she gets started on something.'

'We're going to need lots of help on the day,' said Mandy. 'So I'll let you know, OK?'

'Fine,' said Betty. 'I'll see you both soon.' She stood by the gate as Mandy and Mr Hope drove away.

Driving through the village Mandy spied James

heading towards Animal Ark with a bundle of paper under his arm.

Mr Hope stopped the car to let Mandy out and she ran across to meet him. Mr Hope waved goodbye to his daughter and drove off.

Mandy told James about her visit to see the owl. James unrolled one of the notices to show her.

'Wow, James, it's brilliant,' exclaimed Mandy.

'My dad helped,' said James. 'Then he went to his office to make all these photocopies.'

Mandy was so pleased she felt like giving James a hug. Then she thought better of it. She didn't want to embarrass him. James always blushed

Save Our Sanctuary!

WELFORD ANIMAL SANCTUARY

DESPERATELY NEEDS YOUR HELP

COME TO THE

GRAND NOVELTY VILLAGE PET SHOW

TO BE HELD IN

THE VICARAGE GARDEN ON SATURDAY

by kind permission of the Reverend Hadcroft

CLASSES FOR ALL PETS, BIG AND SMALL

THE FUN BEGINS AT 2 PM

furiously whenever anyone gave him a hug.

'Come on,' she said instead. 'Let's take them round the village.'

'What? You mean put one in everyone's door?' James said looking dubious. 'It'll take ages and we've got lots of other things to do.'

Mandy looked crestfallen. 'Well, who else is going to do it?'

James looked thoughtful. 'I don't know.'

Across the road, Clare McKay, the doctor's daughter, was coming out of the post office. She waved to Mandy and James and came across to talk to them.

'Hi,' she said brightly. She held up her weekly animal magazine. 'I've just been to pick this up. The paper-boy forgot to deliver it this morning.'

Clare had been shy and hardly talked to anyone when she first moved to the house next door to James. But she adored animals and James and Mandy soon made friends with her. Together, they had managed to set up a refuge for a family of hedgehogs Clare had found living in her garden.

'What are you two up to?' The little girl stared at the bundle of notices under James's arm.

Mandy told her and unrolled one so she could have a look.

'Wow, that sounds brilliant!' Clare said excitedly. 'May I bring Guy and Sooty?' Guy was a blind hedgehog Clare looked after and Sooty was Clare's pretty pet rabbit.

'Of course,' said Mandy. 'And tell all your friends about it. We want as many people as possible, and animals of course. We need to raise five hundred pounds at least.'

Clare's eyes widened. 'Five hundred pounds!'

'Yep,' said James. 'So we need all the entries we can get. It doesn't matter what it is – pig or parrot, we'll have a competition for it.'

Clare giggled and skipped away. 'I'll tell Mum and Dad,' she called. 'They've got loads of friends with pets. They can all come.'

When Clare had gone, Mandy looked thoughtful. They still hadn't solved the problem of getting the notices out. Then, suddenly, she had a brainwave. She pulled at James's sleeve. 'Come on, I've just had the most brilliant idea!'

Before James had time to ask what it was, Mandy dragged him rapidly off in the direction of the post office.

Seven

The post office doorbell clanged loudly as Mandy and James hurtled through the door.

'Yes, my dears,' said Mrs McFarlane, the postmistress, as they dashed in. As well as being the village post office, the shop sold all kinds of things like groceries and milk and birthday cards, needles and cotton. In fact, if you couldn't see what you wanted on the shelves either Mr or Mrs McFarlane would go out the back, rummage around, and likely as not come up with what you wanted.

Mandy thought the shop was a bit like Aladdin's cave – full of hidden treasures. Best of all, there

were jars full of old-fashioned sweets like mint
humbugs, butterscotch, aniseed balls and delicious
tangy sherbet lemons. The shop also supplied daily
papers and that was what had given Mandy her
brilliant idea.

'What can I do for you this fine and sunny day?'
Mrs McFarlane was saying. 'A quarter of sherbet
lemons, is it?'

Mrs McFarlane always had a smile for Mandy.
She and her husband had known her since she
was a toddler and were very fond of her. Mrs
McFarlane wore her greying hair drawn back in a
bun and always had on a blue gingham overall. In
fact, Mandy often wondered if she had any other
clothes at all. She had spied Mrs McFarlane in
Walton market once and she *still* had that blue
overall on!

'No, no sweets today, thanks, Mrs McFarlane,'
Mandy said hastily. 'We want to ask you a favour,
don't we, James?'

'Er . . . yes,' said James although Mandy hadn't
yet told him what her idea was.

Mandy took one of the notices and unrolled it
for Mrs McFarlane to see.

' . . . and you see,' she said after explaining
about the show, 'I wondered if you would pop

one of these into everyone's paper.'

At first Mrs McFarlane looked a bit dubious but then she brightened up. 'A pet show, eh? That sounds fun. Well, Mandy, I'd say yes straight away but Mr McFarlane's gone up to Scotland to visit our daughter. I'm on my own in the shop this week.'

'Oh,' said Mandy, feeling disappointed. 'Does that mean you won't be able to?'

'Not really,' Mrs McFarlane said. 'But you'd have to come and put them inside the papers yourself. I have to mark them all up you see, with people's names and addresses so the paper-boys and girls know where to deliver them. That takes a long time.'

Mandy turned to James. 'We can come and put them in ourselves, can't we, James?'

'No problem,' said James.

'The only snag is . . .' Mrs McFarlane hesitated.

'What?' said Mandy. 'We'll come and do it, honestly we will. It doesn't matter how early in the morning.'

'Five o'clock?' said Mrs McFarlane.

'Oh, you mean the day before,' James said innocently.

Mandy nudged him. 'No, silly. Mrs McFarlane

means five o'clock in the morning. Don't you, Mrs McFarlane?'

Mrs McFarlane smiled at James. 'Mandy's right, I'm afraid, James. The papers come at five and they have to be all marked up and ready for the boys and girls at six.'

James gulped. 'Oh,' he said in a funny voice. 'Five o'clock in the morning. Er . . . yes, that's fine, Mrs McFarlane.'

'Yes,' said Mandy. 'Absolutely fine.' She sounded confident but deep down she was not quite sure how she was going to get up that early herself. But it was no good worrying. There was a job to be done and they'd better do it.

Mrs McFarlane held out her hand. 'You leave those with me then and I'll see you in the morning.'

James gave Mrs McFarlane the notices.

'We'll keep one to give to Gran,' Mandy said, pulling one from the bundle. 'She belongs to a club in Walton and I'm sure she'll put it up on the notice-board.' She dragged James towards the door before he changed his mind about turning up so early in the morning. 'Thanks.'

Outside James looked a bit upset. 'How am I ever going to get up at *that* time of the morning?'

'Set your alarm, silly.'

James raised his eyebrows. 'I know *that*, but what's my mum going to say?'

'She won't mind. She knows it's for a good cause.'

'I hope you're right,' James muttered.

'Of course I'm right,' Mandy insisted. 'Now we've got to ask Jean about that tent!'

Back at Animal Ark, Jean Knox was studying the appointments book. She looked up as Mandy and James burst through the door.

'Simon said you know the lady who runs the scouts,' Mandy said. 'Could you ask her if we could borrow their marquee for the pet show, please?'

'Pet show?' Jean frowned. 'What pet show?' She took off her glasses and let them dangle on the chain round her neck.

'We're having a pet show to raise funds for Betty's sanctuary,' Mandy explained patiently. 'And we need a tent in case it rains. Please could you ask Mrs Browne for us?'

Jean raised her eyebrows. 'A pet show?'

Mandy was beginning to feel impatient. 'Jean, will you ask Mrs Browne for us or not?'

'Just as soon as I've got a minute,' Jean said.

'And if you two promise to keep out from under my feet today, I might even persuade her to let you have it for free.' There was a twinkle in her eye.

'Oh, thanks, Jean!' Mandy's eyes shone. Everyone was being so kind. Mr Hadcroft, Mrs McFarlane and now Jean Knox. Mandy had a feeling the Grand Novelty Village Pet Show was going to be a terrific success!

'Prizes next,' said James, studying the list when they got back outside.

Mandy's face fell. 'Oh, yes. Prizes. Come on, let's see who we can ask.'

The village street looked sleepy in the morning sunshine. One or two people were heading towards the post office but Mandy didn't know them well enough to ask them to donate prizes.

They sauntered along by the village green hoping someone they knew might suddenly appear.

'It does seem a bit of a cheek,' James remarked.

'What does?'

'Well, just asking people to give prizes. Maybe it isn't a good idea after all.'

'What shall we do then?' Mandy said dejectedly.

But James had no ideas either. He ran his hand

through his hair. 'I honestly don't know,' he said, looking down-hearted.

But Mandy refused to be beaten. 'Let's take Gran her notice,' she said. 'She might have some suggestions.'

James hurried to keep up with her.

Across the green they could see a familiar figure heading towards the Fox and Goose. It was Mark Boston. They swerved across the green and ran to greet him.

'Hi, you two,' he said, grinning broadly. 'Thanks for bringing Sheba back with your dad this morning, Mandy. Sorry I missed you.'

'Is she OK?' Mandy asked anxiously.

'A bit groggy but she had a little walk round the garden. Or should I say a *limp* round the garden. Thanks again for your help yesterday, Mandy.'

Mandy was just about to ask him why he looked familiar when someone called him from inside the pub. He waved his hand. 'See you two later,' he called, disappearing inside.

Mandy bit her lip. It really was bugging her. Next time she saw Mark she really would find out.

'Come on, James,' she said. 'Let's find Gran.'

They made their way over to Lilac Cottage. The sweet smell of the lilac tree wafted towards them as they went up the front path.

Indoors, Gran was sitting at the kitchen table surrounded by guide-books and maps.

'Where's Grandad?' Mandy asked when she'd given her grandmother a quick hug and kiss.

'Out on his bike somewhere,' Gran said. 'He muttered something about cycling into Walton to get some greenfly spray. His bedding plants are being eaten alive.'

Mandy sat down beside her grandmother and peered over her shoulder. 'What are you doing, Gran?'

'Planning our holiday,' said her grandmother.

'Oh, Gran, you're not going away?' Mandy said in a horrified voice. 'Not before the show!'

Her grandmother patted Mandy's hand reassuringly. 'Not until the summer, darling. We're doing a tour of Scotland in the camper and I'm just planning the route.'

'But Gran, that's ages yet.'

'Nonsense,' said Gran. 'It'll come round in no time and I like to be organised, you know that.'

Mandy grinned. That was typical of her gran. She'd been known to organise her spring-cleaning before Christmas had even come and gone. 'Oh, Gran, I'm pleased you're not going away, yet. We need some more help with planning the show.'

Gran closed her notebook and gathered up the books and maps. 'As a matter of fact, I've been having some thoughts on that too. I've decided I'll run a cake stall.'

'What a brilliant idea!' James exclaimed. Gran's delicious cakes were sure to raise a lot of money.

'And your grandad's decided to dig out that old bran-tub out of the loft and we'll have a lucky dip. Think that's a good idea?'

'Gran, it's brilliant! What would we do without you?' Mandy gave her another hug.

'I've no idea.' Gran winked at James over the top of Mandy's shoulder.

James unrolled his notice. 'Could you put this up in your club in Walton?' he asked. 'Mandy said you probably would.'

Gran admired James's handiwork. 'Did you do it, James?'

'Well,' James went red, 'my dad helped a bit.'

'It's excellent. Yes, of course I'll put it up at our club. 'We've got a meeting tomorrow. I'll take it along with me.'

'Thanks,' said James.

'And we wanted to ask you about prizes.' Mandy said. 'Any idea where we could get some?'

'I could make a special cake,' Gran suggested.

'That's a good idea, Gran,' said Mandy. 'But you'll be so busy baking cakes for the stall you might not have the time. We've only got until Saturday.'

'That's true,' said her grandmother. 'If I come up with any bright ideas, I'll let you know. Meanwhile you could ask in the village shops. They might like to donate something.'

'Now that *is* a good idea,' Mandy got up from the table. 'I knew I could rely on you, Gran.'

They left Mandy's grandmother to finish planning the trip to Scotland and wandered along the street. At the end of the path that led to the cottages behind the Fox and Goose they saw Grandad's friend, Walter Pickard, sitting in his front garden. One of his cats, Missie, lay asleep on his knees. The other two, Scraps and Tom, were curled up beside his chair.

'Hey, let's go and tell Walter about the show and ask him if he'll donate a prize.'

They ran up the path and told him their news.

'That sounds like fun,' Walter said. 'I might even enter my three beauties.' He stroked the ginger cat purring on his knee. Mr Pickard adored his three cats.

'Trouble is,' Mandy said with a frown, 'we need

some prizes. I don't suppose you can think of anything, can you, Mr Pickard?'

Walter stroked his chin with his broad, callused fingers. You needed broad, strong hands to pull on the bell-ropes. 'Young miss, you could have a bunch of my champion roses,' he said, tipping his old cap to the back of his head.

Mandy could smell their sweet scent wafting up from the rose bed beside the cottage.

'Oh, thanks,' said Mandy. 'That would be lovely, Mr Pickard.' Walter Pickard's beautiful cabbage roses would make a great prize for a grown-up, but Mandy couldn't see a youngster being very pleased with them. But she wouldn't have hurt Mr Pickard's feelings for the world.

Walter sucked thoughtfully on his pipe. Then he took it out of his mouth and popped it, still smouldering, into the top pocket of his old gardening jacket. 'And I *might* be able to come up with something else,' he added mysteriously. 'Just leave it to me. I'll see what I can do.'

Mandy gave a sigh of relief. Walter wouldn't let them down. It looked as if everything was falling into place at last.

They said goodbye to Mr Pickard and wandered back towards Animal Ark.

Coming the other way was Ernie Bell. Ernie was a gruff old man but he loved animals and that made him all right in Mandy's book. He was the only person she and James knew who had a pet squirrel. He kept him in a huge run that he had built in his back garden. Mandy and James often took Sammy titbits and loved watching the little creature's acrobatics. They *had* to tell Mr Bell about the show. Sammy would make a perfect entrant for the most unusual pet category.

'I hope he's in a good mood,' said James as they hurried across the road to meet him.

'So do I.' Mandy pulled a face. Mr Bell could sometimes be very grumpy although Mandy knew that under that harsh exterior there was a gentle heart.

'Hi, Mr Bell,' Mandy called cheerily as they ran over. She had learned long ago that the best way to deal with Ernie Bell was to give him her brightest smile and ask about Sammy the squirrel and Tiddles, his cat.

Ernie peered at them from under bushy eyebrows.

'How's Tiddles?' Mandy said, ' . . . and Sammy? I haven't seen either of them for ages.'

'They're fine,' said Ernie, looking from one to the other.

'Have you heard we're having a pet show to raise money for the animal sanctuary,' said Mandy.

Mr Bell frowned. 'A pet show? What kind of a pet show? Not like that Crufts affair where people dress up their animals like dog's dinners.'

Mandy giggled. 'No, not at all. This is for all kinds of pets, not just dogs.'

'Sounds like a lot of nonsense to me,' said Ernie. 'Why can't you just go round knocking on doors and asking for money? Plenty of other people do.'

'Because we want people to have fun too,' Mandy explained. Ernie Bell was always grumbling about something – the weather, the cost of living – but he didn't really mean any of it.

'Hrrumph,' said Ernie. 'What exactly does Betty Hilder need the money for anyway?'

'Mostly repairs to the buildings,' Mandy said. 'Some of them are almost falling down.'

'Hrrumph,' Ernie said again. 'She hasn't asked me.'

'Asked you what?' said Mandy.

'If I could repair them,' he said gruffly. Ernie Bell had been a fine carpenter in his day and still did a bit of woodwork from time to time.

'Oh!' said Mandy, taken aback. 'Would you?'

'I might,' said Mr Bell. He drew himself up to his full height. 'If she asked me I might. I'm not past doing a few repairs you know. I'm a fine carpenter. Best in the county.'

'Oh, yes, I know,' Mandy said hastily. 'I could ask Betty if you like.'

Mr Bell shook his head. 'No, thank you. I'll discuss it with her myself. When do you say this show of yours is?'

'Saturday,' said James.

'Hrrumph,' said Ernie. 'Don't you go interfering, you two!'

'No, Mr Bell,' Mandy said meekly.

When the old man had gone, Mandy jumped for joy. 'I bet it wouldn't cost five hundred pounds if Ernie Bell did it,' she said.

'He might even do it for nothing,' James said. 'Then Betty could use the extra money for animal food or something.'

A broad grin spread across Mandy's face. 'James, I've got a feeling we might be helping Betty in more ways than one. Come on, I'll race you to the butcher's shop. We can ask Mr Oliver if he'd like to donate a prize.'

She sped away across the green. James was hot on her heels.

Mr Oliver was just closing for lunch. Mandy averted her eyes from the bloodstains on his apron. She never ate meat if she could help it. But she knew lots of people did and a prize of a joint of beef might be just the job.

'I'd be glad to, Mandy,' said Mr Oliver when he heard her request. 'Betty does a grand job at that sanctuary. It would be a shame if it had to close.'

James and Mandy crossed the green towards Animal Ark. Mandy's heart was singing. It had been a great morning. All they needed now were more prizes, the marquee, a few more people to lend a hand on the day. The task of organising the show was almost done. But, of course, the most difficult thing remained. They had to find someone important to present the prizes.

Back at Animal Ark Jean Knox was shutting up shop for lunch. Mrs Hope had gone into Sheffield to the veterinary suppliers and Mr Hope was still out on his calls. Mandy helped Jean carry her shopping bag to the car.

'I telephoned Mrs Browne,' Jean told Mandy. 'You can have the marquee for nothing.'

Mandy hugged her impulsively, almost squashing

her glasses that still hung round her neck. 'Thanks, Jean. We've had a terrific morning. Everyone's been really kind. Mrs McFarlane's letting us put notices in all the papers, Walter Pickard's lining up some prizes and Ernie Bell might even repair Betty's buildings for her!'

Just then a magpie flew down, squawking, from the tree in the Hopes' front garden. Jean gave an exclamation of dismay. She flapped her hands about.

'Shoo, shoo.'

The bird gave another harsh squawk and flew off in the direction of the church. Then it circled

and came back. It landed on the roof of Animal Ark and sat looking down at them like a king in his castle.

'That's bad luck, you know,' said Jean, slamming the car boot.

'Why?' asked James.

'There's an old saying about magpies. One for sorrow, two for joy.'

Mandy pulled a face. She loved magpies with their beautiful greeny-black and white feathers and their long tails. 'I don't believe any silly old saying,' she declared. 'I think magpies are beautiful.'

Jean got into her car. 'Mark my words,' she said grimly through the open window. 'Seeing a magpie brings bad luck.'

They watched her drive away.

'Sounds like a lot of nonsense to me,' said Mandy, imitating Ernie Bell's gruff voice.

But James didn't think it at all funny. 'I hope she's wrong,' he said gloomily. 'If this show's going to get off the ground, we're going to need all the *good* luck we can get.'

'It's going to be great, James. Don't you worry about any silly old saying,' Mandy said confidently.

James brightened up. 'OK,' he said with a grin. 'I'd better go, I've got to give Blackie a bath. He rolled in something smelly this morning when I was taking him for a walk. Mum's tied him up in the garden and won't let him in until he's had a wash.'

'Trust Blackie,' Mandy said. 'Don't forget to set your alarm in the morning!' she shouted as James set off for home.

'I won't!' he called back cheerfully.

But Mandy wasn't sure if James would be quite as cheerful at five o'clock the next morning!

Eight

Before evening surgery, Mandy phoned Mr Hadcroft to tell him about the arrangements they'd made so far.

'It all sounds wonderful, Mandy,' said the vicar. 'Let's hope the weather's fine.'

'We've lined up a marquee,' said Mandy. 'The scouts are letting us have theirs for nothing.'

When Mandy put the phone down, Mrs Hope came through into the hallway.

'I've got to go to Twyford Farm to see a sick calf, then call into the sanctuary with some eardrops for Betty's cats. Do you fancy coming?' she asked.

'I've been there once already today,' said Mandy.

'But I'd love to go again. Betty was hoping to put the owl in a flight cage and I'd really like to see him.'

'Right,' Mrs Hope said briskly. 'Get your coat. It looks like rain.'

'What's wrong with the calf?' Mandy called, dragging her coat off the peg in the hall.

Mrs Hope was getting her bag. 'I can't be sure until we get there,' she called. 'Tom Hapwell just said it seemed very weak.'

They drove quickly through the village, over the bridge, and took the narrow road up towards Twyford Hill. Across the vale, ominous black clouds gathered. A dark curtain of rain seemed to be hanging from the sky in the distance.

Mandy peered anxiously through the windscreen. 'I hope it clears up by Saturday.'

'Jean tells me you fixed up a marquee,' said Mrs Hope.

'Yes,' said Mandy. 'But we want to set up parade rings outside if we can.' She glanced at Mrs Hope. 'It's going to be great, Mum. I'm really getting excited.'

Her mother smiled and patted Mandy's knee. 'Betty will be so pleased if you manage to raise lots of money.'

'Yes,' said Mandy.

'I've got a bit of good news for her anyway,' said Mrs Hope.

Mandy's eyebrows shot up. Betty certainly could use some good news. 'What?' she asked.

'I've found a home for the Shetland pony,' said Mrs Hope.

'That's great, Mum!' Mandy's eyes shone. 'Where?'

'One of the women in my yoga class,' her mother explained. 'I met her in the village and she wants a Shetland for her little girl.'

Mandy couldn't wait to tell Betty.

As they approached Twyford Farm, Mandy chatted on excitedly about the show, only stopping when the car bounced over the cattle grid and into the farmyard.

A young man was mucking out the barn with a tractor and loader. He stopped the engine and jumped down from the cab. He wore green overalls and a black woolly cap. It was Mike Hapwell, the farmer's son.

'Hi, Emily. Hi, Mandy. Sorry to drag you all the way up here but I'm really worried. The calf's out of one of Dad's prize milkers. He and Mum are away on holiday and I'll really be in for it if they get back to find it's died.'

'Right, let's take a look at it,' Mrs Hope said in her usual businesslike manner. She took her bag from the car and headed towards the cattle shed.

'No, it's in the house,' Mike said quickly. 'I've put it by the stove to keep warm.'

In the farmhouse kitchen, a thin, newborn calf lay in front of the stove in a huge cardboard box.

Mandy's heart did a somersault. The calf really was poorly. It was thin and shivering and looked half-dead already. Mike had covered it with a blanket and it lay with its head resting on the edge of the box.

Mandy bent down beside the calf. Its eyes were dull and lifeless. She had the horrible feeling their visit might have come too late.

'I found her in the corner of the barn,' said Mike. 'The mother had lost interest. Can you save her, Emily?'

Mrs Hope opened her bag quickly and took out a thermometer. She took the calf's temperature. By now, it was shaking violently. Mrs Hope held the thermometer up to the light.

'It's extremely high,' she said, looking grim. She glanced up at Mike. 'Don't look so worried,' she said. 'It's when the temperature's really low you have to start panicking. This means she's fighting some kind of infection. Get me a syringe please, Mandy.'

Mandy took a syringe from its sterile wrapper and handed it to her mother.

'It's probably caused by the calf not sucking her mother's milk soon enough after birth,' Mrs Hope explained. 'That means it hasn't taken in any natural defences.' She quickly gave the calf an injection in its flank. 'This is serum,' said Mrs Hope. 'It'll give her the necessary antibodies. Another one please, Mandy.'

Mandy handed her mother a second syringe. Mrs Hope gave the sick calf a second jab. 'This is antibiotic to help fight the infection. You should see some improvement by later on tonight. If not, let us know. I'll call again tomorrow.'

Mrs Hope shut her bag and stood up.

'Thanks, Emily,' said Mike.

Mrs Hope glanced at her watch. 'Come along, Mandy. No time to waste.'

Mrs Hope went outside to wash her hands under the yard tap. Mandy stayed behind, murmuring words of comfort to the sick animal. 'Please get well,' she whispered. She covered it up gently with the blanket then hurried outside.

By the time she got to the car Mrs Hope had already started the engine.

They drove along the narrow hill road to the sanctuary. The gate was closed and locked just as it had been earlier in the day. Mandy's heart gave a leap. By this time next week, she thought excitedly, it could be open again!

Betty came out to meet them and unlock the gate and they drove through.

'Hello again, Mandy. I've put the owl in that flight cage round the back. Why don't you go and see him while I talk to your mum?'

'Thanks, Betty!' Mandy ran round the back of the bungalow.

The tiny owl looked dwarfed in the huge flight cage. The cage was about three metres high and four metres long. Inside, Betty had placed some logs and a branch of a tree that had come down in a high wind during the autumn. The owl was almost hidden as its speckled brown plumage mingled with the colour of the wood. In fact, Mandy couldn't see him at all at first. It was only when he blinked his huge, black eyes that she spied him sitting on the highest branch.

'Hello, Mr Owl,' she called gently, catching her breath. It was great to see him sitting up there, almost as if he was sitting in a branch of a tree in Monkton Spinney.

On the ground below, Betty had placed two tiny dead chicks from the chicken farm.

Suddenly she heard Betty's voice behind her. 'I'm hoping he'll come down and get them when he's hungry enough,' she said. 'He'll probably hop down at first but when I get him over to Longmoor, there'll be other owls and he'll learn to fly with them.'

Mandy turned to her, eyes shining. 'He looks much better, Betty. Thank you so much. He's obviously happier now he's out of your office.'

Betty put her arm across Mandy's shoulders. 'I phoned the centre today. They're looking forward to having him.'

'When are you taking him?' Mandy asked.

'Probably early on Saturday morning.'

Mandy would have loved to have gone with Betty but there were so many things to do for the show.

'I probably won't see him again then.'

She peered into the cage. 'Bye-bye, Mr Owl.' Her voice broke with a sudden feeling of sadness. 'Good luck.'

'Don't be sad, Mandy,' Betty said. 'It'll be great to know he's being looked after by experts.'

Mandy nodded. 'Yes,' she said. She knew they were doing the right thing.

Just as they were saying goodbye, the phone rang.

Betty picked up the receiver. She began shaking her head. 'No, I'm sorry, Mike, I can't.'

The person at the other end said something else. Betty went on shaking her head. 'I'm sorry, I just haven't got the funds.'

Betty put the phone down. She turned to Mandy with tears in her eyes. 'That was P.C. Burton from Walton police station,' she said. 'Someone's brought in a dog that was turned out of a car on the motorway.'

Mandy gasped. 'Oh no! How could *anyone* do such a horrible thing?'

Betty shrugged. 'It happens a lot,' she said. 'Tiny puppies often grow into great big dogs and people get fed up with them.'

'But to turn it out on the road,' Mandy cried. 'It could have been killed!'

Betty shrugged again. 'I sometimes think that's what people intend,' she said grimly. 'Anyway, I told Mike Burton I couldn't take it in.'

'Where will it go?' asked Mandy anxiously.

Betty shrugged. 'He's going to try the RSPCA.'

Mandy stamped her foot. 'If I met those people I'd turn *them* out on the motorway,' she declared. 'See how *they* like it.'

Mrs Hope put her arm round her daughter's shoulders and gave her a hug. 'Try not to take it to heart, Mandy.'

'I can't help it,' Mandy said furiously.

'Well, Mandy,' Betty said. 'If your show's a success perhaps by next week I'll be able to take in stray dogs again.'

'Oh, I hope so,' said Mandy. 'I do hope so!'

Mandy felt angry about the abandoned dog all the way home. At a quarter to five the next morning, she didn't feel much better. She hadn't slept very well. Plans for the show were whirling round in her mind. And when she did drift off to sleep she kept dreaming about magpies and calves and Mrs Parker Smythe screaming at the sight of a mouse.

When her alarm went off Mandy jumped out of bed. She had warned her parents she would be getting up early. She dressed hurriedly. She went downstairs, grabbed a banana for breakfast, and crept out of the house.

The village looked tranquil and still in the early

morning light. The sun was just rising, turning the rooftops a deep orange. *Red sky in the morning, shepherd's warning,* thought Mandy. She hoped *that* saying wasn't any more true than the one about the magpies. The shops and houses looked beautiful and peaceful in the clear, still morning light. It was almost as if the world had stopped turning and Welford was frozen in time.

Mandy suddenly froze in her tracks. She drew in her breath, and stood still as a statue. Across the green, a large fox was rummaging about in the bin outside the post office. Its head had disappeared inside. It emerged with something that looked like a half-eaten bun in its mouth. Mandy hardly dared breathe. The fox glanced round furtively, then sat on its haunches chewing.

Mandy remembered a fox her dad had treated once up at the animal sanctuary. It had caught its leg in a snare. It would have died if it hadn't have been for Betty's sanctuary.

The fox's ears shot up as if it had heard a noise. Then, suddenly, it was gone, a red shadow disappearing up the road. It jumped a fence into someone's garden and disappeared.

Mandy saw the reason for the animal's sudden flight. James was plodding across the green, looking half asleep. His hair was tousled, his jumper on back to front. Mandy didn't like to tell him. He didn't look as if he was in a very good mood.

'Good morning,' she said brightly.

James blinked behind his glasses. 'Is it?' he grumbled.

'Cheer up,' Mandy said, falling into step beside him. 'You can go back to bed when you've done the papers.'

James grunted.

Although it was only five o'clock, the post office was already a hive of activity. Mrs McFarlane was sorting the newspapers into piles, writing house names and numbers on each one.

'Do you do this every day?' Mandy asked in disbelief. The thought of getting up at five o'clock *every* morning filled her with horror.

Mrs McFarlane went on sorting the papers. 'Yes,' she said. 'Every day except Sunday. Then the papers are later arriving.'

'What time do they come on Sundays?' James asked.

'Half past six,' Mrs McFarlane said cheerfully. 'We get a bit of a lie-in that day!'

James wrinkled his nose and ran his hand

through his hair. Getting up at half past six didn't seem to be much of a lie-in to him!

'Here.' Mrs McFarlane fished out the bundle of notices from under the counter. 'I've numbered that pile over there.'

Mandy and James began to place one notice inside each of the daily papers. By the time the paper-boys and girls turned up, the task was finished. Mrs McFarlane put a stack of papers into each of their delivery bags and they set off down the street.

James sat down on Mrs McFarlane's stool. He still looked bleary-eyed.

'There!' said Mandy. 'That didn't take long, did it? Thanks, Mrs McFarlane!'

'You're welcome,' the postmistress said. She reached up and took a box of chocolates off one of the shelves. 'I heard you need prizes for your competitions. Will this do?'

Mandy drew in her breath. 'Wow! Thanks, Mrs McFarlane. That's really kind of you.'

Mrs McFarlane went with them to the door. 'My husband will be home by Saturday so I'm going to take the afternoon off and come to your show. I'm bringing Billy. Will there be a class for him?'

Billy was Mrs McFarlane's green budgie.

'Oh, yes,' said Mandy. 'There's a prize for the most talkative budgie.'

Mrs McFarlane laughed. 'Oh, dear. I'm afraid he only says "Pretty boy". But he whistles like the kettle and imitates the sound of the doorbell!'

'Well, that will count as talking, I'm sure,' said Mandy. 'Please bring him along. We'd love to see him. Wouldn't we, James?'

But James had wandered off down the street.

Mandy hastily said goodbye to Mrs McFarlane and ran to catch him up.

'I'm going back to bed,' James mumbled.

'OK,' Mandy said with a grin. 'See you later. Don't forget there's loads of work to be done yet!'

James yawned again and went off groaning.

After breakfast, Jean Knox popped her head round the kitchen door. Mandy was washing-up.

'I saw Mrs Browne last evening. They're taking the marquee over to the vicarage on Friday,' she said.

'Thanks,' Mandy said gratefully. 'I'll go and tell the vicar.'

The surgery was full up as Mandy went through. She stopped to talk to one of the elderly Spry twins, Miss Marjorie. She was sitting huddled up in one corner with Patch, her cat, in a basket beside her.

Marjorie lived with her twin sister, Joan, at The Riddings, a large, gothic house with a long drive and wide, sweeping lawns. It had been Mandy who had persuaded them to adopt Patch when he was an unwanted kitten.

It was unusual to see Miss Marjorie at the surgery and Mandy felt a pang of concern.

'I hope Patch isn't sick.' Mandy peered into the basket.

Miss Spry's face gave a birdlike twitch. 'She's been fighting,' she said in a hushed voice as if it was something to be ashamed of. 'She's a real little spitfire, I'm afraid.'

'I'm sure Dad will soon fix her up,' Mandy reassured the old lady.

Mandy went on to tell Miss Marjorie about the show. 'Do enter Patch,' she said. 'She's such a lovely little cat. I'm sure she'd win a prize.'

Miss Marjorie looked shocked. 'Oh, no,' she muttered, shaking her head. 'Kitty might catch something from the other pets!'

Mandy couldn't help smiling. 'I'm sure she won't do that. Do come along, Miss Spry. Everyone would love to see you.'

Miss Marjorie looked surprised and pleased in spite of herself.

'Oh . . . I'll have to ask my sister.' The twins *never* did anything without consulting each other.

Mandy left Animal Ark and ran over to the vicarage. As she passed the Old School House, Eileen Davy was just coming out with a shopping basket over her arm. Mrs Davy was a violin teacher and gave lessons to children in the village and in nearby Walton. She closed the garden gate and smiled when she saw Mandy pass.

'Hello, Mandy! I got your notice in with my paper,' she said. 'How are the plans going?'

'Fine thank you, Mrs Davy,' said Mandy. 'Everything's almost fixed. We just need to organise the prizes and find someone famous to present them. Your don't know anyone famous, do you?'

Mrs Davy smiled and shook her head. 'No, I'm sorry, I don't. You need someone *really* special to draw the crowds.'

'I know,' said Mandy. 'But who?'

'Have you asked Mrs Collins? She's just about our most well-known resident.'

Mandy nodded and explained why Mrs Collins couldn't come.

'How about Amelia Ponsonby?' suggested Mrs Davy. 'She thinks of herself as a bit of a celebrity.'

Mandy pulled a face. 'Oh, Mrs Davy, we don't want to put people off!'

Mrs Davy laughed. 'No, you're right. Having Amelia present the prizes might be a bit of a problem. To be honest, Mandy, I can't think of *anyone*.'

'Never mind,' Mandy said with a sigh. 'Maybe we'll think of someone. Although we haven't got much time.'

'Well,' said Eileen, 'If I do, I'll let you know.'

'Thanks,' Mandy said. It was great to know people were so anxious to help.

'Would you like a dozen new-laid eggs from my hens to give as a prize?' Eileen asked.

Mandy's eyes were wide. 'Oh, yes please.'

'I'll bring them along on Saturday morning.'

Mandy watched Eileen bustle off down the street, her shopping basket over her arm. Mandy ran off towards the vicarage. All they needed now was for Walter Pickard to come up with some more prizes and someone to present them. Then everything would be perfect!

Nine

Mandy made her way round to the back garden of the vicarage. Mr Hadcroft was in his shed, mending a puncture in his bicycle tyre. He looked pleased to see her.

Mandy told him all about the plans for the show.

'The only thing is,' said Mandy, 'we still need someone really special to open it.'

The vicar ran his hand through his dark curls, then he shook his head. 'The bishop *might* have done it,' he said. 'But it's a bit short notice.'

Just then, James turned up with Blackie.

'Come in and have some tea and biscuits,' said Mr Hadcroft, 'and we'll work out where we're going to put the tables and things.'

In the tiny kitchen, with its old-fashioned gas cooker and scrubbed table, Mr Hadcroft's tabby cat, Jemima, was asleep on a chair by the window. She got up and stretched as they came through the door. Blackie liked cats. He went to sniff her. But Jemima wasn't very fond of Blackie! She arched her back, her fur standing on end. A low growl came from her throat. With a laugh, Mandy scooped the cat up in her arms.

'Blackie won't hurt you,' she said reassuringly. 'Shoo, Blackie,' she said to the Labrador. 'You're scaring Jemima.'

James helped Mr Hadcroft make a pot of tea while Mandy sat by the fireplace with Jemima on her lap. She stroked the cat's soft fur. Then her fingers felt something underneath, on her tummy. Mandy frowned. There was a large lump growing just below Jemima's ribcage. She felt a stab of fear and her heart turned over. Lumps could be very dangerous.

'Did you know Jemima's got a lump on her tummy?' she said to the vicar. Mandy tried not to sound too worried. She knew how much Mr Hadcroft loved his little cat.

Mr Hadcroft looked shocked. 'No, I didn't. Do

you think it's anything to worry about, Mandy?'

'I think Mum or Dad should take a look at her,' Mandy said.

'Oh, dear,' Mr Hadcroft said, his face full of concern. 'I can't take her today, I've got some people coming for confirmation classes. I don't suppose . . .'

Mandy knew what he was going to say.

'Of course I'll take her,' she said. 'Have you got a basket?'

'Yes, under the stairs. I'll get it.'

He went out and came back five minutes later with a huge, old-fashioned cat basket.

'The previous vicar left it,' he explained. 'Will it be OK?'

The basket looked big enough to carry a half-grown tiger in, let alone a cat!

'What did he keep here?' said Mandy 'A lion?'

The vicar chuckled. 'No, I think he had several cats and used to take them away on holiday with him. Can you manage it between you?'

'I'm sure we can,' said Mandy.

When they had finished their snack they went back out into the garden.

'They can put the marquee up here,' said the vicar, standing in front of the bay windows.

' . . . and tables here,' said James. 'My dad's got three wallpapering tables we can use. I've already asked him.'

'Brilliant,' Mandy said.

'And you could mark out the parade rings here,' the vicar said, indicating a broad strip of lawn. 'I've discovered some stakes and rope in the shed. They'll be just the job.'

Before long, they'd decided exactly where everything would go.

'All we need now is people and their pets,' said James.

'They'll come,' said the vicar confidently.

'Especially after that wonderful notice you sent out. How could they resist?'

Back indoors, Mandy put Jemima gently into the basket. 'I'll take good care of her,' she said to Mr Hadcroft.

'Yes, I'm sure you will,' he called confidently. But when Mandy turned to wave goodbye, Mr Hadcroft was standing at the gate with his head bowed. Mandy felt a rush of pity. A cat like Jemima was such a good companion and Mr Hadcroft would be lonely without her.

But behind her confident words, Mandy was very worried. If Jemima had had the lump for a long time, it could well be too late to treat her!

Back at Animal Ark, the magpie was sitting on the gate. It flew off as Mandy and James came up the road. It settled on a high branch in the chestnut tree and stared down at them.

Mandy waved her hand. 'Hello,' she called.

James looked at her as if she'd gone mad.

'Well,' Mandy said, shrugging. 'If by any chance he *does* mean bad luck, we'd better be nice to him, hadn't we?'

They went inside and Mandy settled Jemima carefully into one of the animal cages at the back of the surgery.

Simon was there getting ready for early afternoon patients. Mandy explained why she'd brought the vicar's cat.

'Let's hope it's nothing too serious,' he said. He went to tickle Jemima under the chin.

When Mrs Hope came in, Mandy told her what was wrong. She and James watched while her mum examined the cat thoroughly. Mandy's heart turned over as she saw the frown on her mother's face.

'It's not an abscess,' said Mrs Hope. 'It's a tumour of some kind. I'll have to remove it and send it off to the laboratory in Sheffield. They'll be able to tell me if it's serious or not. I'll ring Mr Hadcroft to ask his permission and find out if she's had any food recently. I can't operate until twelve hours after she's eaten. Put Jemima back, please, Mandy.'

Mandy picked up the cat, cradling her soft fur against her cheek. She felt close to tears. She stroked Jemima's soft coat and placed her gently in the cage. She went out to the office, where her mother was telephoning Mr Hadcroft.

'Mum,' she said bleakly when Mrs Hope put the phone down. 'It doesn't mean Jemima's going to die, does it?'

Mrs Hope gazed at her daughter. 'I'm sorry,

Mandy. I really don't know until we've got the results of the biopsy.'

Mandy felt tears come to her eyes. 'Couldn't you give her some medicine?'

Mrs Hope shook her head. 'Mandy, if Jemima has cancer we'll try to treat her, of course. But maybe, in the long run, the kindest thing would be to put her down.'

Mandy's heart sank. It seemed so cruel. Jemima was only a young cat and should have many happy years ahead of her.

'We couldn't let her suffer, now could we?' said Mrs Hope. She put her arm round Mandy's shoulders.

Mandy shook her head. Her mother was right, of course. She fought back tears for a minute. Then she squared her shoulders and sniffed. 'Sorry, Mum,' she said. 'I'm OK now.' She heaved a big sigh. 'Where's James got to? We've got work to do.'

James was in the kitchen, sitting at the table with pen and paper.

'Right,' he said. 'We'd better write out a programme of events for the show.'

They had just finished scheduling the events when Mr Hope came in.

'Oh dear, Mandy,' he said, putting the kettle on for a cup of tea. 'I'm afraid the weather forecast is pretty bad for the weekend. Rain all day Saturday.'

But Mandy refused to be down-hearted.

'We'll just have to hold the whole thing in the marquee,' she said. 'Anyway, the weather forecasters are often wrong.'

'True,' said Mr Hope. He rubbed his beard. 'Let's hope they are this time then.'

That afternoon, several people called at Animal Ark with prizes for Mandy and James.

Mr Oliver brought the joint of beef. And minutes later, the grocer arrived with a box of groceries. Then Ernie Bell turned up.

'Here!' He thrust a bundle of something into Mandy's hand when she answered the door.

'What is it?' she asked, a bit taken aback.

'Rhubarb,' said Ernie. 'That woman at the post office told me you wanted prizes. Will that do?'

'It's lovely,' Mandy gulped. 'Thank you.'

'You're welcome.' Ernie turned abruptly and strode off down the path.

'Thank you, Mr Bell,' Mandy called after him. Mandy felt very grateful but couldn't really imagine anyone being pleased with a bundle of rhubarb as a prize. Perhaps Grandad could use it for his lucky dip.

'Come on,' she called to James and Blackie. 'Let's take it over to Lilac Cottage.'

On the way, they met Mark Boston. He was taking Sheba out for her first walk since her accident. This time he had her firmly on a lead although poor Sheba, hobbling along on three legs, didn't look likely to run off anywhere.

'Hi, you two,' Mark called. 'What do you think of the old girl then?'

Mandy crouched down to stroke her. 'She still looks a bit down in the dumps.'

'She'd win the prize for the bravest dog,' James piped up.

Mark frowned. 'What do you mean?'

They explained about the show.

'Didn't you get a notice in your paper this morning?' asked Mandy.

Mark shook his head. 'We don't get a daily paper. My uncle says the news makes him feel depressed. What's it all in aid of then?'

Mandy quickly told him about Betty and the animal sanctuary.

Mark's eyes widened. 'And it's got to close, you say? Wow, that's a real shame.'

'It's more than that,' Mandy said glumly. 'It's a disaster!'

Mark shrugged his broad shoulders. 'What can I do to help? Just say the word.'

'I don't suppose you know anyone famous, do you?' Mandy asked. 'We need someone to give out the prizes – someone that'll make *everyone* want to come to the pet show.'

'Huh?' said Mark raising his eyebrows. 'Someone famous?'

'Yes,' James said enthusiastically. 'You know, a film star or something.'

'I might,' said Mark, smiling mysteriously. 'I'll let you know.'

Just then, a white mini-bus pulled up outside the vicarage. Half a dozen scouts got out and began to take out a huge canvas marquee from the back. Suddenly they stopped unloading the tent and stared across at Mandy and James. Mandy recognised a boy from her class at school and gave him a quick wave. To her surprise, he ignored her and just went on staring.

'I'll see you guys later,' said Mark setting off back in the direction of Moon Cottage. He seemed to be in an awful rush.

Mandy and James hurried along to Lilac Cottage

with their bundle of rhubarb. Mandy hoped Ernie wouldn't mind them giving it to Grandad for his lucky dip stall.

A delicious smell of baking greeted them as they went in the back door. Gran was there, up to her eyes in home-made cakes. Mandy could hear her grandfather talking to someone in the sitting-room.

'Yummy!' Mandy said, eyeing the worktop covered with sponges, biscuits and apple pies. She went to take a closer look.

'Hands off!' Gran warned, smacking her fingers. 'You can buy one with your pocket money at the show if you want to.'

Mandy laughed. 'I will – I promise.'

Blackie's nose was level with the table-top. It was quivering. He licked his chops then barked, looking up hopefully at Mandy's grandmother.

'And keep that dog away!' Gran warned again. She shooed Blackie outside.

Grandad and Walter Pickard came through from the front room. Walter had a small cardboard box under his arm.

'Ah,' he said when he saw Mandy and James. 'Just the folk I wanted to see.'

Mr Pickard handed Mandy the box. What on

earth was it? Not more rhubarb she hoped. But no, the box was too small and too heavy.

She gazed up at Walter with shining eyes. 'What is it?' she asked excitedly.

'Open it and see, young miss,' Walter said in a mysterious voice.

Mandy carefully pulled up one of the flaps. She gave a loud gasp of surprise. Inside were rosettes – red, blue, green and yellow. She looked at Walter.

'They're lovely. Thanks, Mr Pickard!'

'Look underneath,' Walter said.

Mandy peeled back the rosettes. Underneath them lay something else. Two rows of sparkling medals. They had 'Welford Pet Show' engraved on one side. Mandy picked one up and turned it over. The other side was engraved with the words 'First Prize'.

Mandy's hand flew to her mouth. She looked at Walter, her eyes wide with surprise. 'Wow, thanks Mr Pickard. They're absolutely wonderful!' she exclaimed breathlessly. 'Real medals! They're just brilliant! Look, James!'

'Glad you like them, young miss,' said Walter. 'I thought they were just the job.'

'Where on earth did you get them?' asked Mandy.

Mr Pickard explained. 'My son runs a sports shop in Sheffield. He popped them over last evening.'

Mandy put the box down and ran to give him a hug.

'Oh, thanks, Mr Pickard. You're so kind!'

'Steve was pleased to donate them,' Walter said. 'He's keen on animals too. He might even come to the show with his Great Dane. It's huge. Have you got a competition for the biggest dog?'

Mandy shook her head. 'No, we haven't, but there'll be something for him to enter. Oh, I do hope he comes. Then I can thank him for these gorgeous medals.'

'I'd better take Blackie home and feed him,' James said when he had looked at the medals and rosettes. 'I think these cakes are just about too much for him.'

'Come on, James,' said Walter Pickard. 'I'll walk back with you and you can tell me all about this show of yours.'

'Thanks again!' Mandy called as they left. She sat down at the table with a sigh.

'Everyone's being so kind,' she said. She picked up one of Gran's magazines and began idly looking through it. Suddenly, something caught her eye. She stared and stared.

'Hey, Gran, look!'

There, on the page giving details of the latest hit records, was a picture of Mark Boston! He looked very different – blond hair combed in front of his eyes, a pink leather jacket and tight jeans. But is was definitely him.

Underneath the picture the caption read, *Mark Sparke, leader of Blue Moon.*

'Of course!' Mandy exclaimed. 'His latest single's in the charts. How stupid of me not to recognise him. No wonder those scouts were staring. *They* knew who he was!'

Gran peered over her shoulder. 'Who?' she said, peering at the photograph.

'Don't you see? It's Mark, Mr Moon's nephew. I *knew* I'd seen him somewhere before! Mark Sparke's his stage name!'

She went on to tell her gran about Sheba's accident.

'Well, I never,' said Gran. 'You know, I like that band.'

'Blue Moon,' said Mandy. 'He must have taken the name from his uncle. Fancy someone as famous as that staying in our village!'

'What luck,' said Gran, wiping a smear of flour from her nose.

'He wants to come and live here—' Mandy said. She broke off. 'Oh, Gran, wouldn't it be brilliant if *he* presented the prizes at the show? I thought he looked a bit funny when I asked him if he knew anyone famous. He must have thought I was joking.'

'Well,' said Gran, matter-of-factly, 'if you want him to do it, you'd better go and ask him.'

Mandy leapt up. She would do *just* that!

Mandy ran out of the house and along the high street towards Moon Cottage. She knocked on the door and waited anxiously for it to open. If Mark agreed to come to the show it would be the last of their problems solved. Everyone would want to come and see him and the show would be a terrific success – better than they ever dreamed of. She shuffled her feet. *Hurry up, Mark,* she said to herself. *Oh, please hurry up!*

Suddenly the door opened and Mr Moon stood there in his painting smock. He held a paintbrush in one hand, a rag in the other.

He looked surprised to see her. 'Oh, Miss Hope. How nice. Have you come to see my studio?'

'Um . . . no, actually I've come to see Mark. Is he in, please?' Mandy said quickly.

Mr Moon shook his head. 'I'm so sorry, he's

just gone tearing off to Walton. He's always in such a hurry, that boy. He leaves me feeling quite exhausted.'

'Do you know when he'll be back?' Mandy asked, her heart sinking.'

'Sorry,' said Mr Moon. 'He didn't say.'

Mandy told him the reason for her visit.

Mr Moon looked doubtful. 'He's going back to London tomorrow. I'm sorry, Miss Hope.'

Mandy couldn't hide her disappointment. 'Thanks, Mr Moon.'

Mandy began to walk away, head down. She felt so disappointed, she could cry.

She heard Mr Moon calling her name.

'Please wait a moment, Miss Hope. I've got something for you.'

Mr Moon came back with something under his arm. 'Here,' he said. 'I've been hearing about your pet show. Would you like to give this as one of the prizes?'

Mr Moon thrust a picture into Mandy's hands. She looked at it and gave a whistle. 'Mr Moon! Are you sure?'

It was a painting of Sheba as a puppy. She was sitting on the patio beside a clay pot full of bright red geraniums. Mandy thought it was the best painting she had ever seen.

'Yes, yes, of course I'm sure,' said Mr Moon, scratching his scalp with the end of his paintbrush. 'I got Sheba from an animal sanctuary and I'm only too pleased to help.'

Mandy stuck out her hand for Mr Moon to shake. 'Thank you *so* much,' she gasped. 'We'll keep it for the biggest prize of all.'

'I've actually got a better idea,' said Mr Moon, stroking his beard thoughtfully. 'Why don't you raffle it? It would be a way to raise extra money.'

'What a good idea!' Mandy exclaimed. Then her face fell. 'We haven't got any raffle tickets.'

'I'm sure Mrs McFarlane will find you some,' said Mr Moon.

'Yes, I'll go and ask. Thanks again, Mr Moon.'

Mandy walked along to the post office with the painting tucked under her arm. She tried desperately not to be down-hearted about Mark. They had some great prizes now, all the posters were out, the tent was up in the vicarage garden. Everything was ready.

Mr Moon was right. Mrs McFarlane *did* have a book of raffle tickets. Mandy bought them and hurried home.

Mr and Mrs Hope were both out so Mandy

showed the painting to Jean Knox, then left it in the kitchen for her parents to see when they came in. She took the medals upstairs and put them on her window-sill. She opened the lid. She took them out one by one and laid them in a line along the window-sill. They were so shiny and beautiful, and she felt very lucky to have them. She was determined not to be upset about Mark. Everything else was going well. Still, it did seem a shame that Mark would miss the show.

Through the open window, Mandy saws her father's Land-rover draw up outside. She rushed downstairs to show him the painting.

He came through into the kitchen. 'Wow!' he said when he saw it. 'That's terrific. Where did you get it from?'

Mandy told him.

'That was kind of him. His pictures sell for a lot of money, I believe.'

By the time Mandy and Mr Hope had eaten their lunch and Mandy had done her chores in the surgery, half the afternoon had gone. There had been no word from Mark so Mandy could only think he hadn't got her message. She went back into the kitchen. Mr Moon's picture was still propped up against the fruit bowl. She decided to take it up to her room for safe-keeping.

The box of rosettes was on the window-sill. Mandy suddenly remembered the medals. She had better put those away too.

But, to Mandy's horror, the medals were nowhere to be seen. She was sure she had left them in a long, shiny row on her window-sill. Her heart lurched. Where had they gone?

She put the painting on the bed and hurriedly opened her dressing-table drawer. Maybe she had put them in there? Perhaps her mum had come in and decided to tidy up? But surely they would have heard her.

Mandy flew round the room in a panic. She opened all her drawers, her cupboards. She searched frantically in her desk. She stood in the centre of the room, her hands in her hair. What had happened to those beautiful medals? Where on earth had they gone?

Mandy ran over to the open window. She looked through on to the garden below. Had they fallen out?

She rushed downstairs. Out in the garden she searched high and low. Her dad came out to ask her what she was up to.

'The medals!' Mandy turned a stricken face

towards him. 'They've disappeared!'

They looked everywhere but they couldn't find a single medal.

'I don't understand,' Mandy wailed. 'I left them on the window-sill. I know I did!'

When Mrs Hope came in she searched as well. She took another look in Mandy's room. She peered under the bed, hunted in the cupboards. There was no sign of the medals anywhere.

'Now everything's ruined!' Mandy sobbed. 'What will Walter Pickard think of me!'

'They might turn up yet,' said Mrs Hope, trying to comfort her daughter.

But whatever had happened to the medals was a complete mystery. They had disappeared into thin air!

That night, Mandy hardly slept a wink. The wind howled round the house and rain lashed against the window panes. Mandy turned her head into the pillow with a sob. Everything seemed to be going wrong. There was no one to present the medals and now, no medals to present. Jean Knox had been right when she told Mandy about that magpie. It *had* brought bad luck after all!

Ten

It was the day of the Grand Novelty Village Pet Show. Mandy awoke early. She leapt out of bed and drew back the curtains. Her heart sank. Not only had the medals gone missing, the weather was terrible. Black clouds covered the sky and the rain was coming down in buckets.

Mandy took a deep breath. They'd just have to have the whole thing in the marquee. After all, that's what it was for!

Mandy hurriedly dressed. Everyone knew about the show now. It had to go ahead, rain or shine.

Downstairs, Mrs Hope was laying the table for breakfast.

'Come on, Mandy. You've got a busy day ahead of you.'

Mandy sat down, trying not to look miserable. She toyed with her bowl of cornflakes.

'Eat up!' Mrs Hope put a plate of eggs and toast in front of Mandy's father.

Mr Hope looked up from his paper. 'Cheer up, Mandy,' he said. 'Maybe it'll stop raining soon.'

'It's not that,' Mandy said, staring into her orange juice. 'It's those lovely medals. I wish I knew what had happened to them.'

Mrs Hope put her arm round Mandy. 'I'll have another look later,' she promised. 'Maybe they'll turn up.'

'Thanks, Mum.'

Suddenly, Mr Hope gave a low whistle. 'Hey, Mandy,' he said. 'Look at this!'

He turned the paper towards her. The headline said, *Pop star to present prizes at village pet show.*

Mandy could hardly believe her eyes. She gave a gasp and grabbed the paper from her dad's hands. She quickly read the story. ' "Pop star Mark Sparke is lending his support to a grand pet show to raise funds for the Welford Animal Sanctuary . . . " ' she read aloud. The story went on to give all the details of the show.

Mandy looked up with shining eyes. 'Wow!' she said. 'That must have been where Mark rushed off to yesterday. His uncle said he'd gone into Walton. He must have gone to the newspaper office.' She beamed a smile at her mother and father. 'Good old Mark!' Suddenly the loss of the medals didn't seem quite so tragic after all.

Mandy hurriedly gulped down her orange juice. She took a mouthful of cornflakes. 'I'm just going to thank him,' she called.

'But, Mandy, finish your—' her mother began. But Mandy was gone, rushing down the street and along the lane to Moon Cottage.

Mark answered her knock at the door.

Mandy gave him a bright grin. 'I've just seen the paper,' she panted. 'Thanks, Mark!'

Mark shrugged. 'I'm glad to help,' he said. 'Is there anything else you'd like me to do?'

Suddenly Mandy had a brainwave. 'You could take care of the raffle,' she said. 'Your uncle's given us a lovely picture of Sheba. Everyone will buy a ticket if you're selling them.' Mandy felt herself go red. Now she knew Mark was a famous pop star, she felt a bit shy.

'No problem,' said Mark. 'I'll be glad to.'

'Oh, thanks,' Mandy said breathlessly.

'What time does the fun start?' Mark called as Mandy ran down the path.

'Two o'clock,' she called. 'See you later!'

Skipping back along the road, Mandy realised it had stopped raining. The black clouds were rolling away and the sun was coming out. Her heart gave a leap. Things just might work out!

Up in the chestnut tree, the magpie flew squawking from its untidy nest. It was joined by another one and the two birds flew around in circles before settling back in the tree.

'One for sorrow, two for joy,' Mandy murmured to herself.

Mrs Platt from the bungalows was walking along with her miniature poodle, Antonia. Antonia had been one of Betty's dogs from the sanctuary.

The poodle was looking splendid in a red collar, her coat clean and fluffy. She greeted Mandy with a lick and a wag of her tail.

'Are you bringing her to the show this afternoon?' Mandy asked as Antonia jumped up to say hello.

'I certainly am,' Mrs Platt said proudly. 'I want to give my support to the sanctuary. I'd never have got Antonia if it wasn't for Betty Hilder.'

'It's going to be great fun,' said Mandy, feeling

excited. 'Mark Sparke's presenting the prizes.'

Mrs Platt looked blank. 'Mark who?'

'Mark Sparke, the pop star. Haven't you heard of him?'

Mrs Platt shook her head. 'No, sorry. But never mind, I'm sure all the young people will know who he is.' She looked up at the two magpies squawking overhead. 'Nasty, noisy things, magpies,' she said. 'They're thieves too.'

'Thieves?' said Mandy, puzzled.

'Yes, they love to take shiny things and keep them in their nests. I once heard about . . .'

Mandy frowned. Thieves? Thieves! She suddenly gave a whoop of joy. She threw her arms round Mrs Platt and gave her a hug. Of course! *That's* where the medals had gone. Mandy had left her window open and the magpies had stolen them!

Mandy sped away. 'Thanks, Mrs Platt,' she called over her shoulder.

Mandy ran indoors. 'Mum? Dad? Where are you?'

But the house was empty.

'They've both had to go out.' Jean Knox had just arrived in the surgery and was hanging up her coat. 'Sam Western's got some big emergency on his farm – they could be ages.'

Mandy's mind raced. James's dad would have a ladder. She rushed over to James's house. He was just coming out, on his way over to Animal Ark.

'They've taken the tables over to the vicarage,' he said as Mandy blurted out her story. 'But Dad's ladder is in the shed.' James dashed down the garden path and wrenched open the shed door. 'Come on, let's do it ourselves!'

Together they carried the ladder across the green. Mandy set it firmly against the tree-trunk.

'You hold it,' she told James. 'I'll climb up.'

'Don't look down,' James warned. He squinted upwards.

Carefully, Mandy climbed all the way to the top. The two magpies watched her, their eyes bright against their shiny black heads. With one hand, Mandy held on tightly to a nearby branch. She leaned across. The ladder swayed.

'Be careful,' James yelled from down below.

By now, a small crowd had gathered to watch.

Ernie Bell shook his head. 'She shouldn't be up there,' he said. 'It don't look safe to me.'

Then, as Mandy reached into the nest, her hand came into contact with something. Something round and cold. She picked it up. To her relief, it was one of the medals! She reached in again.

Soon all the medals were safe in Mandy's pocket. A small cheer went up as Mandy climbed carefully back down the ladder.

James patted her on the back. 'Great, Mandy!'

'Come on,' Mandy said. 'Let's get the rosettes and take the whole lot over to the vicarage before they disappear again!'

They took the ladder back, then collected the rest of the prizes. They made their way over to the vicarage.

The garden looked clean and bright after the rain. The grass sparkled and the flowers looked shiny and fresh. Mr and Mrs Hunter had set the tables up along one side of the lawn. The vicar had already staked out the show rings.

They found Mr Hadcroft in the marquee talking to Mandy's grandmother. She was busy setting up her cake stall.

Then Mandy's grandad arrived with his lucky dip tub and a big cardboard box full of prizes. Walter Pickard was with him, carrying a huge bunch of his beautiful roses.

Soon, the whole vicarage garden was a hive of activity. People were bustling everywhere, setting up platforms, arranging prizes on a table.

Mrs Browne popped in with a megaphone. 'I

thought you might need this to announce the classes,' she told Mandy.

'Yes, thanks,' Mandy said. Her face fell. 'Who's going to do that?' she said to James.

'You can,' James grinned. 'I'm going to be busy getting the entries organised.'

Betty turned up in her old station wagon. Mandy and James helped her unload her display boards. They set them up in the marquee.

The morning flew past and soon it was one o'clock. Mandy gazed round. Everything was ready. The tables, the parade rings, posts with arrows pointing to the parade rings and stalls. On a table by the gate was a pile of entry forms for the various competitions. That was to be James's job. He would take the money and write down the names of the entrants. Her heart began to pound. Only an hour to go. She couldn't wait!

Then Mandy suddenly realised she had not seen her parents all morning. Surely they couldn't *still* be at Sam Western's?

She dashed over to Animal Ark, Simon was just locking up as she arrived.

'Simon, where are Mum and Dad? They're supposed to be at the vicarage. The show starts at two and Mum and Dad are the judges.'

'I know,' said Simon. 'I was just coming to tell you. They're still up at Upper Welford Hall with Mr Western. I've got a horrible feeling they're not going to make it!'

Mandy rushed back to the vicarage to tell everyone the bad news.

'That wretched man,' Gran said angrily. 'I bet he's done it on purpose!'

'But what can we do?' Mandy said anxiously. 'We can't have a pet show without any judges.'

'*You'll* have to do it,' said James. 'You know lots about animals.'

'I can't be the announcer as well as the judge,' Mandy said desperately.

But Grandad always looked on the bright side. 'Well,' he said matter-of-factly, 'we'll just have to hope they get back in time, that's all.'

When it was almost time for the show to begin Mandy sat down on a chair beside the marquee. Mark had arrived and was talking to Betty. Gran was standing by her cake stall waiting for her first customer and Grandad was checking his bran-tub to make sure there were enough prizes. James and Mr Hadcroft were waiting by one of the rings with Blackie. Mandy looked down at the pile of entry forms on the table beside her.

Suddenly the church clock struck two. Surely people should be here by now. Maybe no one was coming after all!

Eleven

Just as Mandy was about to give up hope of anyone coming to the Grand Novelty Village Pet Show there came the sound of a vehicle pulling up outside the vicarage. Mandy ran to the gate. A mini-bus was parked outside and people were piling out. Not only people, but pets of all kinds. There were dogs on leads, cats in baskets, budgies in cages.

Mandy's gran had come up behind her. 'Oh, wonderful!' she cried, clapping her hands. 'It's my friends from our club in Walton.' She ran down the path to greet them.

Mandy saw something else. A string of people

walking down the street and across the green towards the vicarage. She recognised lots of them: Mrs McFarlane with her budgie; Mrs Williams with her cat, Walton; Susan Price leading her pony, Prince. There was little Tommy Pickard, Walter's great-grandson, with his hamsters in a cage; Clare with her rabbit and hedgehog coming along with Lydia and Houdini, her prize goat. Behind them came Mrs Markham with Bunty. Then Mandy spied Ernie Bell with Tiddles in a basket and Sammy the squirrel leaping about in a cage.

Mandy's heart brimmed with happiness. There were so many people! She could hardly believe her eyes. To her surprise, Mrs Ponsonby drew up in her large saloon. She climbed out and went to get both Toby and Pandora from the special compartment at the back. Pandora was groomed to perfection. She had a red bow in her collar. Toby wore one the same colour. And Mrs Ponsonby wore a red hat to match. She swayed up the path in a long skirt like a ship in full sail. Even Imogen Parker Smythe turned up in her pink Lycra leggings and white fluffy sweater. Her mother held her firmly by the hand.

'Now watch out for those rats,' Mandy heard her say as they went past.

'I want a rat!' Imogen was saying.

Mandy chuckled. If there was a competition for the most spoiled child, Imogen would definitely win!

Mandy felt full of rapture. It looked as if the whole village had turned up to support her cause. This was going to be an afternoon to remember!

She greeted people as they came in the gate. 'James will give you your entry forms,' she explained, ushering them through. She glanced anxiously over towards Animal Ark. There was still no sign of her mum or dad. James was right. If her parents didn't turn up in time, she would just have to do the judging herself!

But then she saw her dad's Land-rover heading towards the vicarage. It pulled up with a screech of brakes. Mr and Mrs Hope leapt out.

'Mandy,' her mum gasped. 'Sorry we're late. Sam Western kept us talking. He knew you were having the show today. I wouldn't be surprised if he hoped we'd be forced to miss it!'

'Never mind,' Mandy grabbed their arms and dragged them up the garden path. 'You're here now. I think everyone in the whole world has turned up!'

Mandy stepped up on to the platform and grabbed the megaphone.

'The competition for the dog with the waggiest tail is just starting in Ring One,' she announced. 'Will all entrants please take their places.'

About two dozen people and their dogs filed into the parade ring. Mr Hope stood leaning his chin on his hand, watching them walk round. Mrs Ponsonby had left Imogen Parker Smythe in charge of Pandora while she proudly marched along with Toby. As she spoke to him his tail wagged like mad.

'I bet Toby wins,' Mandy said to Mark, who had come up by her side. In his hand he held an old ice-cream carton full of fifty-pence pieces. 'The raffle's going great guns,' he said.

Mandy turned with shining eyes. 'Isn't it wonderful that so many people have come?'

'And it's all thanks to you and James,' Mark said.

'And you,' said Mandy, blushing.

The parade of dogs was still going on. Mr Hope raised his hand. 'That's fine, thank you. I've made my decision.'

'Oops,' said Mark. 'I'd better do my stuff.' Mandy handed him one of the medals from her shoulder-bag. Mark strode into the ring and shook hands with the winner. Mr Hope had chosen a small boy with a Welsh collie whose tail wagged so fast it was just a blur. There was a blue rosette and a dozen of Eileen Davy's free-range eggs for the runner-up.

In the marquee, Mrs Hope was judging the most unusual pet. A row of people were lined up behind one of the wallpapering tables with cages and boxes of all varieties. There were so many to choose from – a child with a stick insect, a huge man in a leather jacket and motorbike boots with a huge, hairy tarantula, a woman with a pet hen, Ernie Bell with his squirrel, Sammy. In the end the prize went to James's friend with the pet wood-louse.

'Her name's Valerie,' the boy told Mark as he presented the winner's medal. Mark grinned and peered into the box. He confided to Mandy later that he couldn't even see poor Valerie!

Mandy was just waiting to announce the start of the rodent with the twitchiest whiskers competition when there was a shout from the marquee. Suddenly Blackie appeared with something in his mouth. After him ran Gran, waving her fist. Then came James, Blackie's collar and lead dangling uselessly from his hand.

'He's pinched a swiss roll,' James shouted, laughing.

Mandy collapsed into chuckles. She laughed louder when Gran came back, dragging Blackie by the scruff of his neck. Blackie didn't look as if he cared a bit – *and* he was licking his chops furiously. By now, Gran was laughing too. She scolded Blackie, then gave in and hugged him. 'You bad dog!' she said, her eyes shining with tears.

James had gone a bit red. 'Sorry.'

Mandy's grandmother put her arm round him. 'Never mind, James. I'll forgive him. One thing about Blackie – he's got good taste!'

Just then there was another cry from the corner of the garden. Mrs Ponsonby was standing on one of the garden seats, her long skirt held up over her knees.

'A rat!' she screamed. 'A rat, Vicar, Vicar, help me!' Poor Pandora was tucked under one arm, Toby under the other. Both dogs yelped and wriggled frantically as a sleek white rat ran round under the seat. Suddenly it shot out. Mrs Ponsonby screamed so loudly her hat fell off – right on top of the rat!

A little girl ran out from the crowd and knelt down on the grass. She carefully raised the brim of Mrs Ponsonby's hat. Two black eyes and a snuffling pink nose peeped back out at her. She

picked up the rat and held it close to her face. 'Naughty Gladys,' she said and kissed its nose. She went off to one of the show tables, still scolding her pet.

When she was sure the rat was a safe distance away, Mrs Ponsonby drew herself up to her full height and stepped regally off the seat. She put her dogs down. They both ran off after the little girl. Mrs Ponsonby bent to pick up her hat. She placed it on her head with a sniff and went off after her pets.

Then Mandy heard an argument going on behind the marquee. It was Ernie Bell and Myra Hugill. Mrs Hugill was chairman of the WI and wasn't used to being argued with.

'I tell you Tiddles is the prettiest cat in the village,' Ernie was saying angrily. 'And she's the best mouser.'

Mrs Hugill waved her umbrella at him. 'Felix caught sixteen mice last summer. I'm sure Tiddles couldn't beat that.'

'Oh, yes—' Ernie began.

But Mandy interrupted them. They sounded like two children in the school playground.

'Both your cats are adorable,' she said, taking each one by the arm. 'Now come on, please don't argue. Everyone's supposed to be having a good time.'

Mrs Hugill looked sheepish. 'Yes, sorry, Mandy.'

Ernie Bell snorted and strode off towards the marquee. 'I'm going to talk to Betty Hilder,' he said.

'He's just annoyed because Tiddles didn't win a prize,' Mrs Hugill said. Then she went a bit red. 'Felix won second place and that nice pop singer presented him with a rosette and a joint of beef.' She glanced over her shoulder. 'He gave me a kiss,' she whispered in Mandy's ear. 'He's a very nice young man.'

'Yes, he is.' Mandy couldn't help grinning. It looked as if Mark was a big hit! People had been crowding round him all afternoon. Last time Mandy tried to count how many had turned up it seemed as if not only had all the village folk come but half of Walton as well!

Mandy went to find her mother. She was talking to Mr Hadcroft.

'I phoned the lab this morning,' she said. 'There's no need to worry about that lump. Jemima's going to be fine.'

The vicar looked relieved. 'Thanks, Emily,' he said gratefully. 'I don't know what I'd have done if it was anything serious.'

Mandy was just about to say how pleased she was to hear the good news when she felt someone tug at her sleeve. It was Betty. Her eyes were shining.

'Mandy, this is the best day of my life! I've just been talking to Ernie Bell and he's offered to repair the animal pens free of charge if I provide the materials.'

Mandy smiled. 'That's great, Betty. He's a really good carpenter. Do you remember that wonderful cage he made for Lucky the fox cub?'

'Yes, I do,' Betty said. 'And what's more Mark has offered to adopt several of my animals. That means he's going to pay for their food and vet's bills.'

'Oh, Betty, that's brilliant!' Mandy's heart was brimming with joy.

Betty gave her a hug. 'Mandy, I'm so grateful to you.'

The rest of the afternoon seemed to fly past. When all the competitions were finished, Mandy and James organised a grand cavalcade of animals.

The pets and their owners paraded into the ring. Susan Price led the way with her pony, Prince. Prince's coat shone. Then came Lydia with

Houdini. Houdini was prancing about and being mischievous as usual. Clare came into the ring with Sooty the rabbit and Guy, her hedgehog, in a wooden box; Mrs Ponsonby and Pandora with Imogen Parker Smythe holding Toby's lead trotted behind.

James was next, trying desperately to keep Blackie to heel. He wasn't having much luck. Blackie kept leaping forward trying to overtake everyone and lead the way. He was determined to be first in something!

The Spry twins came next with Patch, then Walter Pickard with all three of his cats. There was Mrs Platt and Antonia followed by Gran's friends from Walton with all kinds of dogs and cats. Someone had even brought their parrot in a tall wire cage. 'Pretty Polly,' it screamed. 'I'm simply the best!' Everyone burst out laughing.

Mandy stood at the edge of the parade ring. She suddenly realised just how many of the people walking round were her friends. And their pets were her friends too. She felt proud to know them. They had all turned out to support her and James in their bid to save the sanctuary.

Mandy sighed. What a brilliant afternoon it had been!

There was a round of applause as the competitors filed from the ring.

Betty had gone to stand on the platform and was making a short speech. Mark stood beside her, looking pleased with himself. He held a bucket full of folded-up raffle tickets.

'I want to thank everyone for their kindness,' Betty said to the listening crowd.

Mr Hadcroft came up to Mandy. He looked delighted. 'Your grandad and I have just counted the money. We've raised over six hundred pounds. Isn't that wonderful?'

'Six hundred pounds!' Mandy couldn't believe her ears. She had to tell Betty right away.

Mandy stepped up on to the platform and whispered in Betty's ear. Betty's eyes widened with surprise and pleasure. 'Mandy, that's wonderful!' She turned back to the crowd. 'Mandy has just told me we've raised over six hundred pounds,' she announced. 'I just want to thank you all for your generosity. And most of all . . .' she said, beckoning to Mandy and James, ' . . . I want to thank these two young people for all their hard work on behalf of my animals.'

Mandy and James blushed as the crowd clapped and cheered.

'It just remains for Mr Hadcroft to draw the winning raffle ticket,' said Betty.

The spectators fell silent as Mr Hadcroft put his hand in the bucket and drew out a ticket. He handed it to Mark.

Mark unfolded the ticket then looked up with a grin. 'Number sixty-four,' he called. Then he looked on the back. 'Mandy Hope,' he said. He picked up his uncle's painting and handed it to her. 'Well done, Mandy!'

Mandy gasped. How on earth could she have won the painting? She hadn't even had time to buy a ticket. She was just about to say as much when she heard her mother's voice behind her. 'I bought you a ticket, Mandy,' she explained, giving her a hug. 'I'm so glad you've won – you really deserve it.'

'Hear, hear,' said Mark. To Mandy's embarrassment he bent and gave her a kiss on the cheek.

Mandy blushed. She stared at the picture then at her mother. 'Wow, Mum, thanks! I'll put it up in my room.'

Mandy took a pound coin from a tin with all the proceeds in and handed it to the vicar.

'I haven't forgotten my promise,' she said. 'This is for the church roof.'

Mr Hadcroft took it from her. 'Thank you, Mandy. If we're as successful as you've been today, we'll have a new roof in no time!'

As people began filing out Betty took Mandy to one side.

'I took the owl over to Longmoor Rehabilitation Centre early this morning, Mandy,' she said. 'I felt he had been with me long enough.'

'Oh . . .' Mandy felt a pang of sadness.

'I saw Tom Tyrrel, the man who runs the place,' said Betty. 'He said they'll keep him for three to four months, then they'll be able to release him back into the wild.'

'Where will they do that?' asked Mandy. She wanted to know where the owl would be and that he would be safe and happy and free.

'He'll be released in a place called Carter's Wood,' Betty explained. 'It's a site that they survey regularly. They know there's plenty of prey there for owls, and plenty of trees for them to shelter and nest in. Tom said there's no need to worry about him. He'll be absolutely fine.'

Mandy felt tears come to her eyes. She would love to have been there when the owl was released but she knew that the less contact owls had with humans, the better.

James came up beside her and saw her looking sad. 'What's up, Mandy?'

Mandy told him.

'Betty had to take him,' said James. 'He had to be in a proper place so they could get him ready to be released.'

'Yes, I know,' said Mandy. And although she had longed to see him just once again she knew James was right. In a few months, her owl would be free. Free to hunt over the fields and woodlands. Free to feel the air through his feathers and free to live life as nature intended. And after all, if it hadn't been for that pathetic little bundle Mandy had found on their walk in Monkton Spinney she might never have known that the sanctuary was under threat. At least now the tawny owl wouldn't be the very last creature that Betty would save.

The sun was going down as Mandy and her parents walked back across the green towards Animal Ark. The village was tranquil now. All the cars had gone and the shops were closed for the day. Outside the post office, a little black cat sat washing itself by the wall. The church clock chimed six. Mandy felt exhausted but very, very happy. She knew she would never forget the wonderful day that Welford saw its first Grand Novelty Pet Show. Would it become an annual event? After all, the sanctuary would always need funds. She sighed and linked arms with her mum and dad, matching her strides with theirs. Life was just grand!

ANIMAL ARK *by Lucy Daniels*

All Hodder Children's books are available at your local bookshop, or can be ordered direct from the publisher. Just tick the titles you would like and complete the details below. Prices and availability are subject to change without prior notice.

Please enclose a cheque or postal order made payable to *Bookpoint Ltd*, and send to: Hodder Children's Books, 39 Milton Park, Abingdon, OXON, OX14 4TD, UK. Email Address: orders@bookpoint.co.uk

If you would prefer to pay by credit card, our call centre team would be delighted to take your order by telephone. Our direct line *01235 400414* (lines open 9.00 am – 6.00 pm Monday to Saturday, 24 hour message answering service). Alternatively you can send a fax on *01235 400454*.

TITLE		FIRST NAME		SURNAME	

ADDRESS	

DAYTIME TEL:		POST CODE	

If you would prefer to pay by credit card, please complete: Please debit my Visa/Access/Diner's Card/American Express (delete as applicable) card no:

□□□□ □□□□ □□□□ □□□□

Signature ....

Expiry Date: ....

If you would NOT like to receive further information on our products please tick the box. □